EDITION
ESAM

Linn Meret

The Codices of Tyrsenor

Vol. I

Parilar

Author: Linn Meret
© 2011 EDITION ESAM®
Published by EDITION ESAM http://www.edition-esam.de
Typesetting: EDITION ESAM®
Print: EDITION ESAM®

ISBN 978-3-941769-03-8

Cover design: UlinneDesign, Neuenkirchen
Tornado: VictorZastol'skiy, fotolia.com;
Lion: Dennis Donohue, fotolia.com;
Collage: -   Ulrike Linnenbrink, UlinneDesign
Translation: Sandra Alexander

Title of the original version: "Die Codices von Tyrsenor"

WWW.TYRSENOR.COM

Spirit Dreams

Something outside had jarred me awake. Not a sound, but a movement. A shadow in the clouds, a being like a spirit that had peered through my closed eyelids.

I opened my eyes and breathed hard like after a long flight. It wasn't yet light in my room; the morning fog lay like a white veil over the frost.

The image had given me a good scare; I felt as if I had just escaped from a serious danger. But maybe it was just a dream, even if the image had repeated itself for quite a few days now. A spirit that looked at me, and I couldn't tear myself away because it was able to penetrate its way into my head. And so real that I knew it was there for sure.

Sighing, I slowly rose from the warm featherbed. Still trembling from head to toe, I pushed back the covers and slid into my soft slippers. After finishing washing and dressing, I crept down to the kitchen on tiptoes, intentionally skipping the creaky next-to-last step.

My family was not yet awake. Adopted family to be more accurate. I was not here voluntarily. And after my morning scare, these people were all I needed.

Quickly, I set the breakfast table and tied my sneakers so I could leave the house before anyone was able to see me. After pulling the house door closed behind me, I took a deep breath. Finally alone. Finally no longer having the feeling of being watched.

Little white clouds rose from my mouth as I breathed. For the first time this fall, I noticed that the summer warmth had lost its battle against the winter; unrelenting, the cold pressed forward. The night frosts had already come very early this year; it was only the end of September, but the leaves were already falling.

I loved my morning walk before daybreak. It gave me strength for the upcoming day and I could focus on myself and not my adopted family as I was otherwise obligated.

As a small child, I had been given by my mother to the Capuch family and they had taken me in. But not out of compassion or good nature. My mother had offered them a lot of money to take in little Jella, as they had called me. Why she had done that, I still don't know today.

1

I had always racked my brain about my destiny and made up stories, for example, that my parents had to give me up because they were on the move as brave seafarers or on secret missions or perhaps zooming through the universe in a space ship as astronauts.

But after such phantasies had always led to laughter when I brought them up in school, I had eventually resigned myself to not knowing my parents.

Now and then, anyway. At least I no longer spoke to others about my longing.

But even until today I always secretly asked myself why my mother had delivered me to the Capuch family of all people, a completely strange, totally unknown family. And if I were honest with myself, nothing was more important to me than finding out what actually happened back then.

Where were my parents? Why did they bring me to the Capuch family? What had happened? These were all questions that whirled through my head day and night.

My adoptive parents had never really answered my questions about this. I could never find out whether they didn't want to or didn't know the answers themselves. They had palmed the story off on me that my mother appeared to them one day and had offered them money to take me in. Supposedly, she didn't want to see me again and simply wanted to get rid of me and afterwards, she disappeared without a trace forever.

I didn't believe a word they said and since the time I could think, I pondered how I could find out the true story of my parentage.

In addition, it was not going well with this family. They treated me like a foreigner who was sponging off them although they had received money for my care.

From the time that I had learned to walk and speak, I was the personal maid of my adoptive parents, the Capuchs. They constantly thought that my work was the least I could do for their so selfless behavior. But when the housework was done, they left me in peace. That is, they appreciated not having me in their presence for all too long, so that I enjoyed some freedoms. And it had been that way already for many years now.

Like after every morning walk, I scrunched up my face when I remained standing in front of the magnificent house of the Capuchs with the elaborate stucco decoration over the house door. If it were up to me, I would have taken off and never come back, but where could I seek refuge?

The only people I could turn to were Grandma and Grandpa Capuch, Drude and Hakan. At least they were a part of this family favorably disposed toward me. For that reason I had taken them into my heart so that they became Grandma and Grandpa to me even if they were not my real grandparents.

It was a bit strange: My adoptive parents merely tolerated me in their vicinity; however, their parents gave me the feeling of being loved. But otherwise it would have been unbearable.

Every Wednesday after school I visited my grandparents, who lived in a solitary timber cottage outside the city at the edge of the woods and we drank tea. Sometimes Camilla, my adopted sister, came along, too. Then there were neither tea nor stories.

That, too, was strange, because Camilla was their real granddaughter. But it had been like that from the beginning and so we never questioned it.

Camilla wore pink. Pink clothes, little pink anklets, little pink shoes and little pink bows in her pale blond curls. Everything about her was little! She had gotten stuck in her baby age and seemed to have specialized in bewitching everyone with her childish behavior. To which the constant diminutive of her sentences belonged. Simply a princess. Or more precisely a "little princess."

I could well imagine that Grandma Capuch found this behavior off-putting and that she therefore didn't attain a good rapport with her granddaughter.

Because Grandma was practical. That was her byword. Everything connected with her had to be practical, the laundry, the cleaning, the cooking and so forth. Her hairstyle was also like this: simply cut and short and the gray strands never saw hair color. I believe, even a bun would have been too inconvenient for her, and because of that, she just had her formerly long hair cut off at some point.

Sometimes I suspected that she chose her husband, Grandpa Capuch, on the basis of whether he could be "practical."

Because most times, Grandpa was nowhere to be seen. Wearing his old carpenter's coat, he puttered around next to the house in the wooden shed that bordered directly by a wall of rock or mended the fence that

3

surrounded the solitary property at the edge of the woods, or sat silently in the fireplace room and read.

I have never seen a plainer and more unremarkable man than him. He was Grandma's appendage so to say. That was it. Or not quite: When he prepared tea he came to life. Then tea was celebrated like a High Mass. And his tea was really delicious.

There was something that especially linked me and Grandma. That was a passion for storms. Sometimes when it stormed or thundered, Grandma Capuch lent me her hideously green bicycle and I rode after the storm to watch it more closely.

A month ago I experienced perhaps the most suspenseful moment of my storm quest. It was a Wednesday when Grandma Capuch nudged me joyfully.

"Oh, look, Jella!" she pointed out of the window, The sky had darkened so much that it was already dusk in the late August afternoon.

"Don't you want to go out?" she asked with a mischievous grin.

I pressed my lips together and shook my head. Why could I never say what I really wanted?

"Go ahead and take it, Jella, I know full well that you want to go out." Grandma Capuch held out the key to the shed in which the bicycle was safely hidden.

"But..." I began and pointed at the still unfinished dishes.

The old lady laid her wrinkled and yet so soft hand on my arm, winked at me and smiled at me, so that all of her laugh lines were even more visible.

Thankfully I took the key and kissed her on her sunken cheek. Now I had her old bicycle again and found it incredibly thrilling and fascinating to watch the way the forces of nature raged. I pedaled harder to brace myself against the increasingly forceful wind and rode in the direction of the main street.

It was rush hour traffic and most of the working people who didn't live here in Hokksund wanted to get on the highway to Drammen. Everyone wanted to get home as soon as possible. There was a scramble and the irritable mood of the people was nearly physically palpable.

I now regretted having taken the bike because it looked impossible to cross the street alive. But the approaching storm clouds reminded me of my intention.

In the meantime, a solid drizzle had set in, limiting visibility like a wall of fog. I turned on the small radio that I sometimes carried with me, put the earphones in my ear and now pushed the bike along the side of the road.

"*Severe weather is approaching in the south. I advise all motorists not to turn onto the road to the south; a tornado could form. Until this gets you, we will play Pink Floyd for you,*" a slimy radio announcer's voice quipped.

A tornado! How long had I waited for such a weather phenomenon? Most people believed they only occurred in America. But that was not true; in the last few years there had been more tornadoes in Norway than in any other known time period before.

Perhaps that was due to the fact that one simply called them whirlwinds earlier and not until pictures from the U.S. appeared on television did it become clear that these weather phenomena occurred here also.

I was delighted anyway; I had waited so long for this. My euphoria waned when I wanted to turn onto the highway. Cursing, I pounded my right fist on the handlebars. How could I get to the other side of the four-lane race track with this traffic? Just then a space briefly opened between the cars of two stressed out drivers. I reflexively made use of it and ran across the street. The driver behind me, whom I forced to brake sharply, immediately honked in his helpless rage.

But I now pedaled and made sure that I got away because I had only had one end in mind: the road south! Soon I left the heavily-traveled streets behind me, turned and hastily rode in the direction of the surging storm clouds. Luckily, a tornado had not yet formed.

And then, just as I wanted to turn back, I spotted the beginning of a funnel cloud. I was electrified. I dismounted immediately although I should have instead tried to turn around and get to safety. Because a tornado is nothing to fool around with; I knew that.

But I was too fascinated; I wanted to see the drama up close. And so I stood next to grandma's bicycle and saw the long gray funnel glide over the ground.

The clouds of the storm towered into threateningly dark shapes and greedily sucked clumps of earth and grass into the black abyss of the tornado's trunk. Now the tornado churned like a fury over the land and destroyed everything in its path. I felt my hair sticking out in all directions.

Out of fear, I couldn't catch my breath when the stump of the storm suddenly changed direction and came toward me. Yet even now, I did not run away, but remained standing as if hypnotized. In the meantime, it was all I could do to brace myself against the strong gusts. The wind roared in my ears. It suddenly became clear to me that I was situated in the middle of the increasingly accelerating tornado and had to get away as fast as possible.

I still stared mesmerized at the storm while my eyes watered, and I could hardly hold onto the bike any longer; the wind gusts were so strong. But in the moment when I believed that I would be carried away by storm, the tornado suddenly changed direction and left me behind, covered with dust and dirt.

All of a sudden I saw something moving through the clouds that looked like a large animal. At once I was scared to death. Had the storm sucked up a creature from far way and now carried the poor being along with it?
The fate that had almost happened to me suddenly became clear to me.

Gasping out of fear and in shock, I first staggered back to the road with the bicycle. But then I thought I had been taken in by an illusion. Like children sometimes recognize animals in fair weather clouds when they lie on the ground and watch them drift by. I talked myself into believing it. But my stomach told me differently.

My whole body still quivering, I set off on the way back. I had never before had the courage to venture so close to a storm, to witness a tornado up close. I would never forget this!

I awoke from my daydreams when my way home was finished. Like after every morning walk, I disgustedly scrunched up my face as I opened the door to the magnificent house of the Capuchs with the elaborate stucco decoration over the house door.

From time to time I considered whether there wasn't another family who could take me in. Besides Grandma and Grandpa Capuch, there was my best friend Rose, who always stood by me. But even her family would hardly take me away from the Capuchs. Rose's mother had her hands full taking care of her daughter and her two little brothers because she lived alone, I would just make more work for them. So for now, there was no way out, but sometime I would know where my parents had gotten to and then I would turn my back to this house. With these somber thoughts in my head, I went up the steps to the house door.

Family Life

When I entered, my adoptive parents received me with scolding looks, but without really noticing me. They sat at the breakfast table I had prepared and were enjoying the rest of the coffee I had brewed before my walk.

"Good morning!" I put on my most delightful smile, knowing that they would under no circumstances acknowledge it.

Per just furrowed his half bald head, which looked hilarious because the wrinkles ran along his forehead to the top of his chiseled skull, which was surrounded by a salt-and-pepper wreath of hair like a halo.

He was an engineer and owned his own firm with which he had already earned a lot of money. And so that one could see that, too, he wore thick gold chain on his green plaid vest, at the end of which an even thicker gold watch peeked out of the vest pocket.

Per was the nicest of my three housemates. If he was with me alone, he could even be really friendly from time to time, even if he did try to hide it behind gruff remarks.

But in the presence of his wife Carin, he would never have condescended to drop a kind remark toward me.

Without looking at me directly, Carin wrinkled her little nose, making her somewhat protruding ears wiggle. Why she didn't paint them as well? Everything about Carin seemed to be painted: her finger nails, her toenails, her eyebrows, her cheeks swabbed with rouge, her blond hair.

Actually, she looked quite good, perhaps forty years old, had a nice round face, which appeared only somewhat disadvantaged by the protruding ears.

Carin attempted to hide them under her pale curls. She only spared herself the effort in my presence.

My adoptive mother was the smuggest creature I had ever encountered. She didn't walk, she strode; she didn't speak, she lectured; she stuck up her nose, not only figuratively and was always dressed to the nines. Except on Sunday mornings or when no one but me was present. Then she sat in a lilac robe, uncombed, with her legs crossed and bounced her green-gold slippers on the tip of her toes.

Indifferently, I took off my shoes and jacket and turned the coffee maker on once again. The mailbox rattled, and I went to bring in the Sunday newspaper, which I brought to my housemates at the table.

While Per and Carin read the newspaper and slurped the steaming coffee, Camilla came in a pink robe and matching slippers decorated with light pink pom-poms, strutting down the steps.

Her perfectly styled blond hair rested on her slender shoulders and gleamed in competition with the brilliant chain she always wore on Sundays to be admired by her girlfriends. She had the ears and facial structure of her father, the little nose and hair of her mother and she really looked good with it. And she knew it.

Per and Carin smiled brightly at their daughter, who sat down at the table and was halfheartedly picking at her breakfast egg.

"What's wrong, princess?" Carin looked anxiously at Camilla.

Her daughter sighed theatrically and looked at her parents with big, doe eyes.

"I just don't have any appetite."

"But we gave Jella special instructions to prepare a five minute egg for you; she still doesn't remember."

Hellooo!!! That was so untrue.

Every Sunday I cooked a five-minute egg for the little princess, a seven-minute egg for the queen and a ten-minute egg for the king! This family simply couldn't be beaten when it came to misrepresenting the facts. I was furious, although I was already familiar with this pejorative ritual. Carin looked at me disparagingly. For her I was just a servant.

"Kjersti got the same little purse that I just bought for myself last week. And now I can't let myself be seen with her, unless one of us is carrying a different little purse!" Camilla whined on. Reproachfully she looked at her mother, who for her part was staring helplessly at her husband.

"Well, then, just take another purse; you have so many," her father Per ventured to say. Horrified, Camilla cringed.

"What?" she screeched.

"You want me to carry a dirty old purse while Kjersti is dragging a brand new designer purse with her that I could be carrying as well?"

9

"Oh, come on," I said and sat down at the table with a bowl of cereal. "You're perhaps exaggerating a bit; you've got umpteen designer purses that you've only used two weeks or even less. All of them still look completely new."

Camilla's eyes flashed at me and her expression changed to disgust.

"You have no idea about such things, so in your place I would keep my mouth shut. If you absolutely want to have a say, then go to the shopping center and inform yourself about the newest fashion trends, instead of reading any fantasy books about waves or some such thing."

With a clatter I pushed the filled plate away from me.

"They are books about wind and storms and science! And besides they are nonfiction books. The kind that can be found in every good library and not fantasy," I replied, for my part packing my contempt in the sentence.

Camilla just rolled her eyes.

"My God, I get pimples from people like you." With these words she turned again to her parents.

"Mummy, Daddy, can I please get a new purse so that I don't have to be ashamed of myself?"

Carin and Per looked at one another seeking help.

"Darling, I wouldn't buy a new purse right away...maybe you can think..."

"You're taking Jella's side aren't you?" Camilla shrieked.

I sputtered forcefully with a full mouth and the milk I had on my spoon spread out over the whole table.

Aghast, three pairs of eyes looked at me.

"I'll wipe it up," I assured them.

Carin shook her head and answered the incensed Camilla, "No, not at all. But..."

No further argument occurred to Carin. She advocated my opinion, in fact, which she would never admit. And now she sat in a trap like a fly, which was wound up in a spider's web and struggling. I didn't begrudge her...

Even Per, who otherwise always had the last word, sat on his chair as silent as a fish and avoided looking into his daughter's eyes.

"You have the same opinion as her there!" Camilla pointed at me like a judge to a convict. Then she flew from the table leaving her blankly staring parents behind.

After the further silent breakfast, I tended to the laundry. I wouldn't have to clean until tomorrow, so I had the rest of the day to myself. In my room, I sat on my bed and turned on the CD-player.

My room was large and light blue walls gave it a pleasant tranquility. My bed stood to the right against the wall, next to a white nightstand. The likewise white wardrobe took its place at the foot of the bed. A desk complete with chair was located in front of a window, that took up almost the entire front side of the room and through which the sun twinkled in each morning. A full length mirror hung resplendent on the wall next to the door.

At any rate, I had a beautiful room, which I attributed to the payments of my mother twelve years ago. Or was it thirteen years? I determined that I didn't even know precisely.

Longing gripped me again as soon as the thought of my mother came up. Sadly I looked in the mirror. Why couldn't I find out what had happened?

There was no help for it; I suppressed a few tears and decided to work to distract myself from my dismal thoughts.

Toward evening – I was just finishing my homework – Carin pushed open the door.

"We're going to the theater now. Take care of washing the dishes." No knock, no good bye.

After the house door clicked shut, I tiredly stumbled down the steps. They had – like most of the time – eaten the evening meal without me and I felt hungry as a bear. So I warmed up the leftover lasagna. While I munched away it grew dark and the sun shed its last light, illuminating the emerging clouds eerily from below. Shortly after that I went outside to bring in the wash before it began to rain. When the last piece of laundry was in the basket, it already began to drip and I heard rumbling in the distance. A thunderstorm was brewing. That prompted a sense of well-being in me.

Back in the house, the dish water wrapped my hands in pleasant warmth, when the first lightening streaked across the sky. A massive clap of thunder followed.

Interested and already elated, I looked toward the sky when I – briefly illuminated by another bright lightening – caught sight of a winged something. Only for a brief moment, but I had seen it accurately. An eerie catlike being with wings. It was big, as big as a wildcat, a lion or tiger perhaps.

Deeply terrified and confused, I rubbed my eyes.

"You're dreaming, Jella. There is no such thing; you are overworked and tired." I talked to myself and went into my room and collapsed into my bed with weak knees.

The short moment had been enough to frighten me. My whole body quivered and cold crept up my back.

This night I had nightmares, the content of which I couldn't remember and woke up again and again trembling with fear until I fell into a restless sleep close to morning.

Rose

A relentlessly annoying "beep" awakened me. Half asleep I stumbled out of my warm bed. I felt exhausted after the restless night. Six thirty, I had to get ready for school. A cold shower revived me and I began to look forward to seeing my girlfriends again.

But the previous day still gripped me. Above all I couldn't get the peculiar being that I believed to have seen out of my head.

In school, I passed through the long hallways that were imbued in a glaring white by the horrid fluorescent tubes. In the classroom, I took my seat next to the window and waited for Rose. When the bell rang, she burst hectically into the room and sank, breathing hard, next to me, a white rose in her curly hair.

Her real name was Katharina, but everyone called her Rose because she always carried one of these flowers with her.

Differently from Camilla, she did not wear dressed-up clothes with it. Today she had put on faded jeans with a light yellow blouse, well suited to her tanned face and the dark brown hair that fell to her shoulders.

Along with her love of roses, her laugh was her most noticeable feature. She laughed when she was asked something, she giggled when others spoke and she always snorted with laughter at even the least little things.

In her company no one could be sad or downcast for long and even the grouchiest and grumpiest teachers became friendly when they spoke to Rose.

"Hey, are you up for coming home with me after school? We could go walking together or invent our own baked muffins again..." she whispered to me, laughingly batting her eyelids.

Our shared hobby was inventing some kind of muffins that didn't necessarily taste good or sometimes just walking a few laps in the park. That always cleared our heads from all the stuff that they beat into our heads at school.

I would have loved to go home with her to get away from the Capuchs, but I unfortunately had to turn her down.

"Sorry, Rose. Today is cleaning day."

She groaned loudly. "Oh, yes. You are expected at the royal house."

I was just about to reply when our teacher, Mr. Loman – late as always – banged his heavy leather bag on his desk and without delaying himself with a long opening speech, began the morning with complicated arithmetic problems. When the bell later rang for the first break, everyone hastily gathered up their things and hurriedly left the classroom.

"Will you come along tomorrow then?" Rose continued our interrupted conversation, as we made our way to our lockers.

"Yes, tomorrow is perfect. But don't you have your rose class on Tuesday?"

Rose held free 'rose classes' in which she shared her knowledge about roses with anyone interested. I myself had also taken part once and was genuinely proud of my friend. She did a great job.

Rose shook her head. "I moved that to Friday when you have your ironing day. Then we'll have more time for ourselves."

I smiled at her thankfully and hugged her. Rose laughed and shook me off.

"No reason to exaggerate, okay?"

We fell silent as Camilla pushed her way through the crowd with her three so-called girlfriends. I had once overheard these three of Camilla's followers complaining about her behind her back in the girl's lavatory. Probably they only trotted behind my adopted sister because she wore the hottest clothes and had allegedly already had so many relationships with boys. At the same time, she had just turned sixteen.

"Out of the way!"

Camilla forced herself between us and strutted to the schoolyard like a ruler with her little troupe.

Rose rolled her eyes and we disappeared to the one place Camilla was never seen – the library! After school we said goodbye and I marched home.

I opened the front door. Per was at work, Camilla was still at school and Carin, still in her robe, sat in the living room, speaking with a friend on the telephone, nagging at the top of her voice.

First I put on the water for the pasta; then I set the table. While the water was still slowly warming along with the soft hum of the burner, I took a feather duster and began to work. I had already learned early on that dilly-dallying did not get the work done and always began my duties early enough so that I at least had enough time in the evening to take care of my homework.

14

At eight o'clock in the evening I was finally finished and fell into bed exhausted. I had cleaned the whole house, I had freed even the smallest sculpture from specks of dust and even mopped under the carpet. And now I had to deal with arithmetic problems and geometric constructions.

Worn out, I decided to first rest a while, only to come to a new decision to copy from Rose tomorrow. Like always, when I was once again not successful at taking care of my own matters after finishing my forced labor.

The next morning I quickly scribbled a copy of the last of Rose's neatly written answers before the bell rang for the first period.

After school I rode home with her. She lived in one of the ugly row house developments that stood like an impenetrable wall on a dreary suburban street. In spite of the awful façade of the building she lived in, I liked being with my friend. After all, her apartment was wonderfully chaotic. The toys of her little twin brothers Leon and Oskar lay everywhere.

Rose's mother opened the doors and smiled with pleasure when she spotted me. She had the same hazelnut brown eyes and the same smile with the cute dimples as her daughter.

"Jella, nice to see you. I'm terribly sorry, but I need to leave for work and didn't have time to cook something tasty for you. I hope that doesn't bother you."

I had to grin. That's how she always was; always worried when she didn't get something finished, because performing her job as a nurse and then raising three children alone in addition was a big job that one could hardly live up to!

"No problem, we can cook something for ourselves."

Rose's mother nodded, pleased.

"That would be great. Leon and Oskar are still in Kindergarten. Maybe you can pick them up later this afternoon?"

Rose nodded and disappeared with me into her room that she, how could it be any different, had decorated with wallpaper in a rose pattern.

"Sit down." Rose rummaged around in her bookcase and threw a book on the bed next to me.

"The Miraculous Flower Rose" I read aloud.

"I got a hold of it on sale at Jacobs' Bookstore. Isn't that fabulous?"

15

To me, it looked like a quite ordinary new rose book, but I didn't want to chase the glitter in Rose's eyes, so I nodded enthusiastically.

"I know that it's nothing special for you, but for me it is something wonderful and I am overjoyed about it." Rose grinned, and I suspected what would come now.

"Oh, no!" I said, pretending to be indignant more than being honestly put out. In reality I liked going there with her.

"Oh, yes. Come."

She pulled me to my feet and out to the little greenhouse that she was permitted to build in the community garden of the row houses. It consisted of several windows and a wobbly steel frame that we found the summer before last at a junk yard. Several panes had a crack and if a hurricane or tornado would blow in, the whole structure would be doomed.

We spent almost the whole afternoon transplanting roses and browsing in the new 'wonder book.' About six o'clock in the evening I brought to her attention that we should pick up Leon and Oskar if we didn't want to be greeted with loud bawling and tear-filled eyes.

Later in the evening we said goodbye to one another and I trotted home alone in a melancholy mood. The next morning my school day began with English and afterwards science was scheduled.

A clueless teacher

In the classroom, Mr. Bergenson waited for us. Abused by nature with a horrible hooked nose, crooked back and the shrill voice of an old man, he seemed the caricature of a school master in a movie. The same dark gray suit as always hung loosely on his skinny frame and from time to time a musty smell drifted from his corner to us.

First he gave us a lecture about the past classes when he was absent and had received several complaints about us from certain substitute teachers. Then he changed the subject. With a bored voice Mr. Bergenson continued:

"Now, as you all know, the one-week internship will soon take place. I expect you to find a placement by the end of this week." With these words he let himself sink into his squeaky teacher's chair and banged his science book on the desk.

"Do you already know where you're going?" Rose asked me quietly while I tried to inconspicuously move over to her.

"Nope, not yet. I thought I'd try the weather radio. And you?"

"Hmm...Maybe I'll choose the Bengalese Garden in Drammen. I'll see."

I nodded and opened my book to the page number the teacher gave us. The title 'Storms and Severe Weather' jumped out at me and my heart began to beat hard.

Finally! I had been longingly waiting for this topic since the beginning of the school year; I had read so much about it and was eager to learn more about these powers of nature.

"Who can tell us something about hurricanes or tornadoes?"

My hand shot in the air so quickly that I was in danger of falling from my chair, but I held onto the edge of the desk just in time. Curious about the noise, the eyes of all of my classmates were glued to me. But I ignored them and tried to make eye contact with Mr. Bergenson. Unfortunately in vain.

Because he just warned us, ignoring my hand, "If all ladies have now placed themselves comfortably in their seats, I would find it favorable to follow my lesson silently."

"But I -" I began and raised my hand to reveal my knowledge about hurricanes and tornadoes, but was forcefully interrupted.

"You should have gone to the bathroom during the break!" He had completely misunderstood me. Sighing I let myself fall back into my chair.

"Now, a hurricane is a tropical storm that brings winds up to 30 miles per hour~"

"What?" escaped from my lips and I quickly put my hand in front of my mouth.

Mr. Bergenson raised an eyebrow.

"Do you have something useful to add?"

"Yes!" I sat up inwardly.

"Only above 80 miles per hour can one designate a tropical storm as a true hurricane. Above 120 miles per hour it is catastrophic beyond measure. A hurricane has a diameter of up to 100 miles."

I had expected that Mr. Bergenson would quickly correct himself or meekly admit I was right with a scarlet face, but what he did now surprised me.

"If you would at least have something reasonable to contribute to the lesson. But to confuse your classmates without any reason... Something like that makes me angry."

Taken aback I gaped at him. What was that supposed to be? Anyone could look it up in a fact book and then it would turn out that I said the right thing. Confused, I listened to his further remarks.

"Hurricanes occur for months and destroy everything possible in this time..."

I looked at him appalled. What was the old windbag babbling about there? I never knew him to be like that! He had always explained physics and chemistry to us very well. But he seemed to not have the faintest idea about the rest of the natural sciences. He now appeared to me to be completely unaware of the world.

"Hurricanes exist for weeks and their season officially lasts from June 1st to November 30th! These tropical storms can develop everywhere where water is found..."

Wrong again! They develop mainly in the trade wind zone, over the water. The water must be at least 78 F warm.

I almost exploded in rage and close to tears, I buried my face in my hands. My classmates must notice that Mr. Bergenson was just spouting off incoherent stuff!

Seeking help, I looked around, but no one seemed to be listening to the lesson. Everyone was busy with something else, whether it was throwing paper pellets or, like Rose, scribbling something in her notebook.

I was delighted when the class period was over. This teacher had bungled my favorite topic. I swiftly gathered up my things and made sure I got out of the building.

Police

At home, I dialed the number for the weather station to apply for an internship.

"Hello, here is the central weather station of southern Norway, what can I do for you?" came from the other end of the line.

"Hello, here is Jella Capuch. I wanted to apply for an internship, that-"

"No, sorry," the unfriendly voice cut me off.

"There are no internships with us. Goodbye!"

Speechless I stared at the telephone receiver. Well, that was unfriendly! And now what was I supposed to do for an internship?

On Thursday afternoon I still had no internship. Since midday I had asked in every firm and every store, but without success. Now I had just one place to turn that might perhaps have a position available. The land survey firm owned by my 'Daddy,' Per. Ugh...

I had intentionally left this place as the last possibility so that Per wouldn't have to see me outside of the house. But now I had no other option.

On the way to his office, I was just about to rush across the street when a loud honking abruptly stopped me. A police car stood to my left and a hand waved me over to the driver's window.

I swallowed. Did they want to arrest me because... because..., yes, why, actually? I couldn't remember doing anything forbidden.

"I wanted to make you aware that you must wait at a red light until it is green!"

The policeman in the car grinned at me, friendly, but firm. I looked at the traffic light. Oh, I hadn't even noticed it in my frustration.

"Yes, won't happen again. I'm just in a bit of a hurry."

"Can I help you somehow?" the friendly young officer asked me.

"If you by any chance have an internship available, then yes," I retorted flippantly.

"Yes, coincidentally, I have one available," the uniformed officer answered seriously.

I stopped short. "You mean, I could..."

"Of course, you can come anytime. Our station is directly next to the train station. You can register there."

20

"Wow, thanks a lot! I would be coming starting next week."

"Well, then, until next week."

The policeman waved goodbye again and then he raced away with screeching tires. He probably wanted to impress me a little.

Grinning, I strode home. I finally had an internship! I was enthused and above all relieved that I didn't have to beg from my adopted father.

On Monday morning I arrived in the police station at eight o'clock on the dot, after having made all the arrangements with the personnel department the week before and reported to the officer on duty at the gate. There was just enough time for a short greeting in the department where I was supposed to work. A policewoman introduced me to a few uniforms, but the young officer who brought me here was not there. Then the policewoman explained my tasks for the coming days.

I was supposed to work in the archives and help resort the countless files. Great! I had envisioned the internship differently. Something with flashing lights, chasing gangsters and gunfights. At any rate more suspenseful than taking care of some kind of paperwork.

After the first endless hours when it was time for lunch and I wanted to go out into the fresh air, I heard a familiar voice. The policeman who had stopped me was conversing with a colleague in a small side room.

"Ah!" He had seen me and gave me a friendly smile.

"Our new intern! You can help me right after your break. Just come to this room when you are ready."

I felt flattered and raced right into his office after the break. "Welcome, and take a seat." He pointed to a chair in front of him.

"I am Chief Inspector Louis Taperzo." Cordially he offered me his warm, dry hand and I shook it vigorously.

"Jella Capuch."

"Well, Jella. Do you see the cartons there? They are moving boxes. I am being transferred to Bergen and you now have the job of clearing my things off the shelves. There are all kinds of odds and ends that can be thrown out and it would be nice if you would sort it out a little."

I had to swallow my anger. Actually I had now expected to be introduced to the secrets of police work. Instead I was supposed to bring the chaos in his office back into order and play his maid.

21

I had no other choice than to get to work. I emptied books, binders, parts of uniforms, even handcuffs and billy clubs and many other odds and ends into the boxes. Suddenly something similar to a bracelet fell into my hand and I hesitated.

What was that? It was light and in fact looked like a black bracelet. Instead of a watch case there was a rectangular plastic block on a wide nylon band with a clasp.

"What is that?" I asked and held the thing out to CI Taperzo.

He looked up from his paper work, scrunched his eyebrows together and then said:

"...an electronic ankle cuff. Prisoners who are employed or do not necessarily have to be locked up due to family reasons, get an electronic ankle cuff with which they can be located at any time with the help of radio networks. I probably forgot to return it to the properties room. Please lay it on my desk; then I'll put it away later."

I nodded so he knew that I understood and continued clearing out. Toward evening I left the police precinct with sore arms and was more than happy when I finally lay in my pleasantly soft bed.

Uncanny Encounter

In the night I suddenly awoke with a start. What was wrong? Something strange had awakened me again. Something that I still couldn't identify. Had it been a noise, a draft or a light? Uncertain, I stood up and looked tiredly around the room. Through my big panorama window I had a good view of the house door.

Something was moving there. I turned into a pillar of salt. My knees began to tremble; cold fear rose up my back. Down there something was scurrying demonically across the lawn, something big, cat-like, and it now came toward my window. A giant animal with wings. I pinched myself on the arm.

Wide-eyed I gazed at the monster, incapable of moving away. Was I hallucinating? Hadn't I just recently seen something that looked like a cat with wings? With my heart pounding, I crept up to the wide window in order to get a closer look at the creature, which couldn't really exist.

It was as big as a full-grown lion, but with a more slender body build and a longer head. But the most peculiar thing of all: It had wings on its back. Its glossy fur was almost white and shimmered in the pale night.

I pinched myself on the arm again. Was I going crazy? Was this perhaps a fit from the too strenuous hours of cleaning?

This being looked like a white panther with light wings on its sides!

I couldn't catch my breath. My heart beat in my throat; my back cramped up. Wheezing, I rubbed my eyes.

That thing down there; I couldn't be seeing it! I had gone crazy; I was truly mad!

All of a sudden it raised its powerful head and looked straight into my eyes.

Something in my head exploded when our eyes met, and I held my hand on my forehead, groaning. What was wrong with me? Was I still dreaming? A dreadful nightmare, only with the difference that I could feel my bare feet on the cold floor.

And now I also heard the wildcat speaking! I must definitely be going crazy. Because it spoke with its mouth closed; I heard its deep, droning voice in my head.

"You are not dreaming; I am real. I am a luzo and have chosen you as one of my riders."

Why could I now hear the monster? I just now realized that the window that went almost down to the floor was open a crack. A cold draft on my feet brought me back to normal.

Or perhaps not? Because the voice was not in the room; it was in my head! There stood a mythical creature with wings on its back and spoke to me! I almost fainted from fear.

"Ahhh!" I screamed and in my panic I tore the desk lamp off of the table, which hit the floor clattering.

What was going on me? It wasn't normal to hear a foreign voice in your head.

"Calm. Please stay calm." There it was again. The voice.

But all at once, I no longer felt fear, just confusion. What did the being say? It was a luzo?

What was a luzo? Why could I hear its strange sounding voice in my head? And why was the creature here?

As if it could read my thoughts, the voice explained to me, "I am a luzo, for you, so to speak, an animal. An animal that can communicate with you by means of a bond that only exists between the two of us so that no one else can hear what we say to one another."

I automatically looked down at myself, but, as was to be expected, there was no bond to be seen.

What did it mean? Carefully, I stepped closer to the window. The luzo perked up its bushy ears hopefully.

"Will you come down?"

I cringed at the idea of standing across from this being. Yet after a few seconds of fearful consideration, my curiosity won and I gathered all of my courage. I quickly dressed, tiptoed down the steps as quiet as a mouse and opened the house door with trembling hands.

The luzo looked even more splendid up close. It had silky fur and glittering green eyes.

"I am Parilar, your luzo! You have been selected as my rider. That is your and my destiny."

In disbelief, I shook my head. What I saw could not be true! I closed my eyes and opened them again, repeated that again, but the luzo was still standing before me.

24

"What do you mean, you chose me as your rider? And why me?" I stammered, hoarse with fear.

"I didn't simply choose you; one is destined for another. That is the invisible bond. Actually I was designated for someone else, but that must have been a mistake because there was no bond between that person and me like there is between you and me."

"And you are quite actually real?" I asked, still bewildered.

Parilar scrunched up his snout into something that looked like a smile.

"As far as I know, yes. I must surely look foreign and gruesome to you. Actually, riders are only chosen from among our people, seldom or almost never from people outside of our world. I wonder myself how this could happen, but it has come to pass now."

"From your people? Does that mean you come from another world or something?"

"No, not as far as I know. Or not directly. Our people have just distanced themselves from other humans because it must remain secret that we luzos exist. If all people in your world would find out that there are winged cats that can even communicate with you, your whole world view would be shaken and somehow attempt would be made to find a scientific explanation. At our expense, of course. Therefore we hide ourselves."

I had to first process all of that. Trembling, I hopped from one foot to the other. What would happen now?

"You must come with me. My people are waiting; they do not know whom I have chosen. They also don't know where I am. A few weeks ago I just took off from the assembly because something was pulling me to Hokksund." Parilar winked at me kindly.

"Climb on."

Frightened, my eyes flew open.

"Never in my life will I sit on you!"

Parilar groaned and took another step toward me.

"Come on, you must come with me. I won't do anything to you. Trust me."

I still hesitated, weighed his words and looked Parilar over closely. I couldn't find anything threatening about him, though, but saw only a gentle

25

expression and an encouraging blinking. My instinct told me that I could trust him.

There was a special connection, an old familiar bond as if we had known another for a long time. Now I was even using the word 'bond'...

"OK, why not," I sighed. With these words I swung myself onto his back and seated myself gently between his wings. I could hardly believe what I was doing there. It seemed totally unreal.

Now Parilar spread his wings, took a big leap forward, and took a short run in order to then take off. His wings whirred in the soft starlight. We were flying.

Filled with fear, I clung to his short mane and pressed my head against his shoulders. When we were over the treetops, he dropped his flight path a little and we glided gently over the treetops of the Egerskogen, the forest north of Drammen.

Slowly the lump in my throat loosened and my fingers relaxed. I carefully sat up. Cool night air pleasantly touched my hot face.

I just now noticed that I felt as if I had a fever; the adventure up to now had excited me so much. But now a smile stole its way to my lips, and for a short time, I was able to forget the incredibility of this situation.

I just simply felt free!

Luzos and Codices

"Where exactly are you flying to?" I asked Parilar after a while when I was halfway calmed down.

"We are flying to my people and then a ceremony will take place, which will permanently bind us with one another. Because we are the number five that will close the circle."

Confused, I stared at the back of his head.

"What do you mean? Can you now perhaps clarify for me what is happening here?"

With a serious tone, the luzo now spoke to me and I sensed a shudder run over his strong body. Which passed on to me. The hair on the back of my neck rose. Something creepy was happening here.

"You must know that 'the Great Five' exist for us. Those are five luzos with their riders who have the task of protecting the *codices.* If one of the 'Great Five' dies or otherwise is lost, this generation is dissolved, which means that they are no longer the 'Great Five.'

As quickly as possible, a new generation is chosen or someone, who takes the open spot. Which can sometimes take a long time.

Only the luzos of the 'Great Five' are assigned special riders. Because only these pairs have special powers with which they can protect our holy shrines and our community.

We have many luzos and many riders, but not all luzos have the same connection with their riders; although they are close to one another, they could be assigned another rider. When for a long time, no one is found who is connected with a luzo by a bond, the 'Great Five' is incomplete. And that is a dangerous time for us.

The codices can only be sufficiently guarded by the 'Great Five' together.

Now I have found this bond with you. That means quite honestly that both of us are destined to become part of the 'Great Five.'"

"What are the *Codices* then?" I collected my meanwhile trembling voice for a temporarily last question.

"You will find that out when we have arrived and the ceremony has ended," Parilar now answered in monosyllables.

"And what kind of ceremony is it?" Somehow I felt stupid just then. I understood less and less and so I added another next to the last question to my temporarily last question.

"To become a part of the 'Great Five,' a dedication must take place. And I have sent news to our village that we are coming today and the dedication ceremony can take place."

Parilar's words swarmed in my head like flies on a summer meadow. 'Luzos, Codices, the Great Five, riders, ceremonies.' All that was too much for my brain.

In addition, I had lost all sense of time and began to wonder that I was not miserably freezing in the clothes I had hastily slipped on before my flight. It was fall and at the height and speed at which we were moving, I should have long ago stiffened into an icicle.

But I didn't feel the cold; on the contrary, the air felt like a mild summer night.

I fell silent and started to be interested in the land beneath us, because the starlight was bright enough to reveal some details of the area under us. At first, I had seen the lights on the ground along the river, but after we had flown for a time through a white wall of fog that had suddenly appeared, the ground remained completely dark.

We now flew over a landscape unfamiliar to me. The forest had given way to a lake landscape and I believed at first that Parilar's path would be leading us to the east in the direction of Oslo and then further to Sweden. But the lights of the city were not to be seen, the fjord that would have provided a clear marker on the way east from Hokksund also did not show up.

On the horizon, the darkness was already giving way to a delicate veil of light that announced the approaching daybreak. Ahead of this twilight, high mountain peaks rose visibly up into the clear sky. It couldn't be the mountains in western Norway unless the sun meanwhile rose in the west...

These heights before us were in the east and they were also much higher than the peaks between Stavanger and Bergen. Or had mountains grown into the sky in Sweden over night?

"What nonsense," I scolded myself for these crazy thoughts.

Where were we?

I sent this question to Parilar who led me to understand monosyllabically, that we were in another country. It would be better not to know the exact way. This knowledge was the secret of the luzos.

After a while, he shared with me that we had now arrived.

We flew in a gentle half-circle over a clearing in the forest, which spread out to the horizon in a vast basin between high mountains. Houses at the edge of the trees indicated a village, but it was still too dark to determine how big it was. And there were no lights to be seen.

In the soon brightening gray of dawn I discerned a large cluster of people under us on a square, around which spacious flat wooden houses were arranged. When we came closer, I became aware that it was a large community. The extensive square in the center appeared to form the heart of the village. In the distance, in the west, I could recognize a sandy field.

"That is the training ground," explained Parilar who now watched me again.

Skeptically I raised an eyebrow. Something was tingling in my belly. Was it the excitement? The fear had given way to a joyful anticipation on the way to this settlement. What adventure would await me here?

"And the large building is the Luzo Archives, our shrine. There we keep everything that we know about our kind," he continued.

He pointed to a drab structure at the north end of the square, whose highest spire was now already illuminated by the morning sun. It stood on a rocky hill, that towered roughly and forbidding out of the plain, behind which the high mountain peaks reached into the sky. Gray towers on immense blocks of granite dominated over a building that emanated power. The huge gate in the middle was bordered by two giant figures.

Marveling, I took in everything. Then Parilar steered toward the cluster of people. And – yes! There were other luzos to be seen! When Parilar began to land and came near to the assembled people, some luzos rose into the air and remained next to and behind us. These flying beings also carried riders who observed me with curious looks. The luzos were different colors and different sizes. When we had finally arrived below, I dismounted.

A tall older gentleman in a floor length dark gray robe came toward us, and Parilar bowed humbly in front of him. The tunic of the glowering man was fastened in front of his chest by a silver brooch and ended with a hood in the back. His nose looked like a chiseled stone that someone had unintentionally planted on his face. A beak, so to say, not beating around the bush any longer.

The almost white hair of our counterpart made him look dignified, and it was apparent that he was the leader here, because he was the only one to wear a sword on his wide black leather belt. It, by the way, didn't appear that it had been made for battle because its golden handle was decorated with numerous silver inlays; the sheath in which it was inserted bore green and blue stones in golden settings. An oval red stone decorated the top of the handle, which clearly contained something inside that looked like a star. A broad vest and black leather pants gave him a war-like appearance.

"I did not count on your choosing someone else, Parilar. We have been waiting here for you to begin the ceremony and now you bring someone we do not know. Can you explain that to me? Our ancestors have never been wrong, how could that happen?" the leader spoke to my luzo in a loud and enraged tone.

"Our ancestors were not wrong, Zaron," Parilar replied with a humbly bowed head.

"They only prophesied it was someone born under the sign of Saturn and that could be many. Perhaps Corey and Jella were born at the same time on the same day. They didn't exclusively prophesy that it was Corey."

Zaron turned to me.

"Your name is Jella then. Well, when were you born?" he asked with a gruff voice.

I swallowed and managed a feeble "I don't know" with a clenched voice

That was the truth. The Capuchs had explained to me that my birthdate had never been known and they simply made up a date when they registered me for school.

Zaron furrowed his brows and appeared to wait for a further explanation.

"I am adopted. I don't know my birthdate."

He nodded, twisting his face into an annoyed expression and waved to a boy about my age. A big and strong lad, not much older than sixteen, stepped out of the surrounding crowd of people. His black hair stood out from his angular head like little clumps. He looked 'like a simpleton,' as one would have described his facial expression in our school and in spite of the weird situation, I had to suppress a giggle.

"Corey, the luzo assigned to you has chosen another rider. We must respect that. Our winged helpers are those who feel the bond and if it is not strong enough, they can make another choice. But you were trained for so many years; we can't just throw that away. Therefore you will receive a luzo tomorrow in spite of this. But you can no longer be part of the 'Great Five.'"

The boy he had addressed as Corey looked sadly at the ground, but said nothing. Then he nodded and returned resignedly back to the crowd. Somehow I felt sorry for him now.

Zaron now turned to Parilar and me again.

"Jella, what do you know about us? Has Parilar explained to you what lies ahead of you here?" he asked in a snooty tone that annoyed me.

In the process, he just looked at my luzo who must have given him to understand that I knew the facts, because he asked abruptly:

"Are you ready?" and looked at us expectantly.

Parilar lowered his head in agreement before I could even open my mouth.

But I was not ready! Before something happened here, I wanted to spit out all of my questions, know what was going on here, where I was and so forth. What was supposed to come now?

Slowly, fear crept up my spine again and I felt the hair rising on the back of my neck.

"What is happening now?" I asked Parilar in a frightened voice.

"Just be brave; we will now undergo the dedication ceremony which will allow you and me to become part of the Great Five. Don't panic; nothing terrible will happen," he droned.

Zaron turned around without regarding me any further, went to the crowd which parted in front of him and entered a building in the background. When he came out again, he wore a long white robe with wide sleeves the sides of which were covered with strange, embroidered characters, unfamiliar to me, something like:

I thought I had seen this sort of letters once before in school. Was that Old Greek?

31

On his head he had a long, pointed white hat; in both hands he carried an uplifted bowl made of dark wood that was apparently filled with water or another clear liquid. Now he no longer looked like a warrior, but rather like a priest.

While Zaron strode through the crowd, all whom he passed bowed their heads. It appeared that what he held in his hands was holy. When he reached us, he said in a tone that brooked no disagreement, "Follow me."

We went behind him to a small flight of steps that led to a pedestal out of gray stone blocks. On the pedestal stood a column out of black stone, in which the same unfamiliar old characters were carved that I had seen on Zaron's priestly robes. On the front side of the granite column was a small hollow. When I looked closer, it occurred to me that the column was formed like the torso of a woman.

Zaron placed the bowl that he had carried here, into the small hollow, stepped back, raised his hands to the sky and murmured a few words in a language unfamiliar to me.

Parilar and I stood behind him. The people from the village had arranged themselves in a half circle behind the pedestal and kept a respectable distance. No one said a word, no throat clearing or coughing was to be heard. Not even the wind seemed to dare to send a breeze. At a far distance only, a child screamed and a dog barked.

The sun had meanwhile risen and sent its first rays over the high peaks in the background.

All at once, it became clear why the ceremony was taking place now.

At the spot where the planet Saturn had earlier been visible in the darkness, a beam of sunlight now emerged between two high peaks. It fell directly on the column that was now illuminated by the bright light. The rest of the podium remained in the shadows. The engraved characters on the stone now emerged vividly and looked as if they had come off of the column and were floating in the air.

Breathless silence intensified the mystic manifestation from which I could not withdraw myself. No one moved; Zaron, too, stood like a statue in front of the stone and appeared to wait for something. The sun climbed a little higher and in its glow, the letters moved a little in the direction of the bowl.

All at once a sunbeam fell on the surface of the water. It looked as if it would be awakened to life. It rippled a little as if a gust of wind had moved over it. But it was completely calm.

The letters now reflected themselves above it in the small waves and produced a strange pattern that quickly looked like a single large foreign letter. The silvery glowing liquid had all at once turned to pure gold, or so it looked from my vantage point.

The large character into which the unfamiliar letters had united appeared to be engraved; the wave movements had stopped and a bright glow fell on Zaron's face.

He now stretched both hands forward and dipped his fingertips into the liquid that now looked like it was smoldering.

The foreign character floated over his hand. The master of ceremonies now slowly pulled his fingers back. His fingertips were covered with pure gold.

He slowly turned around, raised his hands and stepped toward Parilar and me.

Involuntarily, I closed my eyes. Then I felt his hand on my head. A great heat streamed through me. I tried to open my eyes again, but it wasn't possible. My muscles didn't obey me.

What was all of this here? What was happening? Why did I have no power over my own body? Panic began to spread through my body; I no longer felt my feet and noticed my legs giving way. What had I gotten myself into here?

Zaron said something again, and I noticed how he was moving away from me. I opened my eyes. I was master of my voice again and took a deep breath.

Parilar stood next to me with closed eyelids. A gold streak ran from his forehead over his whole snout to the light tip of his nose.

Now he lifted his eyelids and looked at me from the side. As if drawn by an unknown magic, I stepped up to the luzo. Then I bent forward and our heads touched at the spot where Zaron had marked us.

A while long nothing happened; then a powerful electric bolt flashed through my body. My forehead burned like fire; I wanted to scream and free myself from Parilar, who was now trembling violently.

But we did not come apart from one another. It was as if we had been welded together. We became one being. Energy streamed back and forth between the both of us. My I and his I melted into a blazing wave.

I felt close to fainting; so taxing was this painful process for me.

Helpless as I was, I could not get away from the animal and in my deepest soul, I didn't want to. But it was hellishly painful. Then everything went black, and I felt myself sinking to the ground.

Suddenly drums droned in my head, I saw bright lights and all at once, energy flowed through me like I had never before experienced. Ecstatically I stood up; I felt Parilar and myself changing. I opened my eyes.

Zaron stood in front of us, bowed, threw his head back and shouted loudly with a dignified voice, at the same time raising his hands to the morning sky, "Welcome to the circle of the 'Great Five.' You are bonded and it is your destiny to protect the holy codices and our people. On the day on which you detect your power, you are totally united. Arthrpa bless you."

Jubilation broke out in front of the podium and the people hopped and danced in excitement. The water in the depression in the column now looked as it had before. Namely like water. The sun stood higher in the sky and the mysticism of the ritual gradually faded.

They, that is, Zaron and two of his helpers, led us into a furnished room after the ceremony and thought we should first recover ourselves. I was dead tired and at the same time excited.

After Zaron and his attendants had gone, Parilar lay down on a nest full of blankets and a few minutes later I heard only his regular breathing. He snored.

I was too occupied with the past hours to be able to do the same. I had submitted to everything without being able to register or influence what had taken place. What would Rose think of everything when I told her? Certainly, she would find it totally exciting and would want to know every little detail.

When Parilar was awake again after a short sleep, I had many questions. Some things he could explain to me, but the most part still remained behind a supernatural veil.

In the ceremony, Zaron bathed us like in a baptism with water that he called "Landuza." I also had a golden stripe on my hair after the ceremony, Parilar mentioned.

What was this Landuza once again? It was a holy lake that no one was permitted to approach who was not chosen.

And the characters on the column?

"Ancient," murmured Parilar, still half asleep, "Someone once told me that it was Etruscan, but don't ask me what that is, I can't even read."

And the golden stripe?

"That fades again after the ceremony and remains invisible. But the golden streak also only appears on luzos and people who are joined by the bond."

"What did Zaron mean with Arthrpa?"

Suddenly the luzo jumped up as if bitten by a snake, and startled, I took a step back.

"That is the name of the goddess of destiny. No one is permitted to speak her name; only Zaron is allowed!"

We looked into one another's eyes for a while, and I decided to hold back any additional questions after observing the strange expression in his pupils. While I still continued to ponder, sleep finally overtook me and my heavy eyelids fell shut.

Nightmares

It was pitch-black and I found myself in a room full of spider webs and dust. On the floor lay old crates and broken furniture. Quarrelling voices came out of a wide crack next to a door that led to a neighboring room.

Having become curious, I made a path through the clutter and looked through the small slit. In the neighboring room, I discovered a man with caramel-colored hair and piercing yellow eyes.

In front of him on a half torn-up chair sat another man, whose appearance made me shudder with sorrow. He wore torn clothes; his brown hair was disheveled as if he had lived on the streets for years.

I couldn't recognize his face, but to judge from the facial features of the man with the piercing eyes, they were not conversing about a pleasant topic.

But there was someone else in the room. My breath caught. That couldn't be!

Kneeling on the floor was – I!

It was unmistakable, my long black hair, my posture.

I was just a few years older, a grown woman. The woman who so resembled me sat with her back to me, but I recognized her right away. Was I by any chance looking into the future?

"I'll tell you for the last time. If the two of you disappear from here, or only you alone, Adrian, then nothing will happen. Because the two of you together are as valuable as a clump of dirt; however, you alone are as valuable as a piece of gold." The man twisted his face and smiled lovingly at the woman- me.

"But if the two of you do not accept anything of the possibilities that I'm offering you now ..." He didn't finish the sentence. Instead he pulled a knife out of his coat packet.

The woman – I whimpered distraught and said something to the disheveled man. I could no longer understand the words because everything around me became blurred.

"Jella, wake up!"

Drowsily, I squinted through half-opened eyelids and saw a demonic mug with huge teeth and enraged green eyes in front of me.

I screamed loudly.

Startled, Parilar jumped back, colliding with a table on which a clay jar stood. As if in slow motion, the vessel first began to totter and finally smashed into a thousand slivers on the floor with a loud bang.

Appalled, I held my hand in front of my mouth. Oops. Guiltily, I looked at Parilar, who was still examining me in shock. Then we both began to laugh and soon tears of laughter were rolling down my face when suddenly there was a knock at our door.

"I don't want to disturb you, but if the ladies and gentlemen have calmed down, it would greatly please me to see you dressed, washed and fed at the training grounds."

The voice was not Zaron's; I had never heard it before. I guessed it was that of the older gentlemen. Anyway, it did not sound unpleasant.

"Yes, sir!" cried Parilar submissively and licked his fur. It almost sounded as if my luzo was obliged to obey this gentleman.

"Who was that then?" I asked while I splashed cold water on my face.

"I believe that was our mentor. But I know him as little as you do."

"Our mentor?" I asked with an apple in my mouth.

They had really furnished this room well. Nothing was lacking. I had even found clothing, but it didn't fit me and also looked rather old-fashioned.

Only makeup was missing. And the water was cold. At least there was a water faucet.

Parilar interrupted his cat grooming.

"Yes, he will teach us everything that we have to know and is at the same time our caretaker."

Suddenly I paused, upset. It was broad daylight, and I should have been in the police precinct long ago to do my internship work. Oh, God! What was I supposed to do now? On the one hand I had now been accepted as a luzo rider; on the other hand I still had a 'normal' life.

At this moment, Zaron knocked on the door and I told him that I had to go to the police station in Hokksund without delay.

"That's all we need," he grumbled to himself disgruntled.

"Not only does Parilar drag in a person from the outside, now she has obligations in another world! How is that going to turn out right? Well, then fly off with Parilar, take care of that and then return here afterwards," he snapped.

I was shocked. Zaron was apparently not in agreement with Parilar's choice. But I felt clearly that I couldn't go back. My connection to Parilar was too close for that. We were one; that was clear to me. And how was I supposed to "take care of that"? Could I fulfill both obligations?

"But I can't simply disappear later and what should I tell my adoptive family?"

Zaron scratched his chin pensively. His look did not bode well.

"Hmmm, that could become a bigger problem. Tell me, what's the name of your adoptive family?"

"Capuch."

Zaron's eyes widened.

"Per and Carin Capuch?"

Surprised, I nodded.

"Well, at least one bright spot. Maybe we'll be able to take care of the mess. The Capuchs are acquainted with luzos. Their ancestors themselves were in contact with luzos and they have been guarding the secret for generations. You will explain everything to them," he continued in a harsh tone.

If I it was possible to be any more confused, I was so at the present moment. The Capuchs had something to do with luzos? Not in my wildest dreams would something so absurd have occurred to me. I was now happy to be able to leave the room, and Parilar and I immediately headed for Hokksund.

The flight back to the west went by faster than the outward flight and within the shortest time we again flew into the gray wall of fog that we crossed through on the way here.

Now I recognized familiar landscapes again and the few lights on the edge of the forest of Egerskogen showed us a direct route to Hokksund. Here it was still dark like autumn, as if we had cut off several hours.

In spite of that, I came significantly late to my assignment with the police; however, Louis didn't appear to be angry. He winked at me briefly and said laughing, "...It must have been a little strenuous for you yesterday...?"

Conscience-stricken, I lowered my head and waited for further abuse. He just assigned me new file work however and left me alone until quitting time to complete my tasks.

When I came home, Carin and Per sat together with Camilla at the dining table and ate supper.

I gathered all of my courage:

"Carin, Per, can I speak with you?" I spoke to them straightforwardly.

Astonished, both of them looked up. Camilla made a daft face; she was not accustomed to such audacity from me.

"What do you want? Can't it wait until after the meal?" Per asked irritated. I bit my lip.

"No, it cannot!"

My expression and my tone silenced both of them; now their astonishment changed into curiosity and both of them followed me into the living room.

Per appeared to suspect something, because with a gesture and a harsh command, he ordered Camilla, who wanted to follow us, to stay in the dining room. She pouted, but I saw that her father's tone had triggered respect in her.

"Do you know the luzos?" I launched my question quite abruptly.

Per and Carin became simultaneously pale and looked at each other seeking help.

"Well – how should I say this – I wanted to share with you that I am now a luzo rider." I stammered with an uneasy feeling in my stomach.

I waited anxiously for their reaction and quickly got to hear one.

Carin held her forehead and aghast, Per loudly groaned.

"No! Since when?" Per didn't look happy.

"To be exact, since last night. I am supposed to tell you that I will fly there after the internship with the police and eventually also after school and have to take training classes."

Carin nodded, "I knew that we would not be spared from this luzo stuff forever. Do what you want; it makes no difference to me. As long as you no longer bother us with this stuff."

With these words, she turned on her heel and I stood alone in the room with Per.

"Not a word to Camilla. She is never to find out about this matter," Per snarled at me and disappeared into the dining room behind his wife.

Okay, then, good luck! I closed my eyes and sank into thoughts of Parilar. Inwardly I was calling to him. Deep inside I knew that the invisible bond that connected us would bring the luzo to me.

Then I went through the yard and looked into the sunset. A gentle rustle announced the mythical being and before nightfall, I spotted the silhouette of the winged cat-like being.

I didn't hesitate long, swung myself on him and we flew to our first training class.

The luzo adventure had one good thing at least: I had to spend less time with the Capuchs.

Sagor's School

I had already seen the training grounds from a distance yesterday. It was the large sandy field on the horizon. Many other luzo riders were already assembled there with their animals. They stood in groups of three each: a luzo, a rider and a third person who was clearly older than the riders. I assumed these were the mentors or trainers and was correct in my assessment.

A chubby man with a bald head smiled at me pleasantly. He was surely already sixty or older; his skin was tanned from the weather and deep wrinkles had embedded themselves into his face. He was small and stocky and sported a pretty fat tummy in front of him.

"Welcome, Jella. I am Sagor."

I returned his smile. It was his voice that I had heard in front of our door this morning.

"Will you be our mentor?" I asked him uncertainly.

He quickly nodded and said in his quiet voice, "Yes, I will pass along to you my knowledge about the necessary combat techniques."

Whoa there, did he say combat techniques? I had still been so excited the whole time and had so many questions in my head, most of them unanswered, so that I had hardly given any thought to what Zaron had termed training yesterday. Why 'combat techniques' then?

I had imagined that what was in store for me today would be something like school lessons, perhaps with topics like the history of the luzos or something of the kind. And now wasn't I perhaps supposed to get to know the other fellow riders of the Great Five? And I still didn't know where I was here, who all these people were, why I belonged here and so forth.

"Yes" went through my head.

"Why do I belong here and why do I feel so clearly that this is my destiny here?"

My confusion slowly resolved itself as the many questions began to be organized in my head. I felt that I was at home here although I had seen this village for the first time yesterday. Somehow everything here seemed familiar.

41

Sagor appeared to have seen through me. With a serious face, he turned to me and said:

"Jella, I know that everything at this time is a lot of new impressions. It is understandable that you have hundreds of open questions. We will surely be able to answer all of those for you, as far as we know the answers ourselves.

"But now an emergency has arisen and we cannot lose any time. The Great Five of the last generation were lost a long time ago and since then the village has lost its protection.

"As you know, the 'Great Five' are supposed to protect our Codices. The Codices are the sacred writings that our ancestors bequeathed us. Zaron will tell you more about that someday because he is the only one who knows their importance more precisely. Only so much: A long time ago already there were attempts to steal our hallowed books. And we must prevent that by all means.

"My task now consists of training you as quickly as possible, so that you can be in place with the other four in a battle. We had many omens in the past weeks which suggest that danger threatens our village."

Now I became uneasy. It was grumbling and rumbling inside of me. These were not butterflies; they were ravens hurtling through my stomach. At least. If not even larger creatures...

"But," I began. "But why did you choose me for this and not a professional fighter? After all they could ..."

Sagor didn't let me finish:

"We didn't choose you; you came to us," he said harshly.

"We had already chosen Corey; we wanted to make a heroic fighter out of him. But you and Parilar decided otherwise."

I looked at him dumbfounded. Until yesterday, I had still believed that my arrival here was a coincidence. And that I was more or less supposed to become a sort of high flyer here. Flight demonstrations with Parilar or something like that.

Now quite a few things were going through my head that I had already heard from Parilar. How could I have been so naïve?

The Great Five were endowed with special abilities that they initially didn't know themselves, which would, however, become apparent to them at some

42

time by means of special events. And only five riders together could protect these people. And these riders had to be ready to fight.

How naïve I had been. A moment long I thought of ordering Parilar to bring me home. But then I realized that I felt at home here. Inwardly, I felt that I belonged here and always wanted to be here.

My mind couldn't grasp it yet, but my feeling was far further along. And this feeling was already enough to provide me the confidence that I would soon understand everything that was happening around me. And what task was intended for me. Because I could now sense that I was here on a fateful, predestined path.

Sagor had looked at me the whole time with squinting eyes. And my luzo also stood next to me with laid back ears. The tension was palpable.

"Jella, it is not possible to undo everything," our mentor now said with a serious face.

"Parilar and you, you are connected by the invisible bond. Your luzo did not choose you alone, you found one another. Why you as the only chosen one live outside of our community, we do not know. But now you belong to us. And you know that, too."

I now nodded with a serious face. He was right. There was more than I could grasp with my reasoning power. Everything that was happening here was as it should be and necessary. My body told me as much.

I lowered my head as a sign that I was in agreement.

The tension dissolved as Sagor began to explain our practice plan without further questions. It was quite something. The exercises on the training grounds appeared to require much agility, endurance and speed. I could already tell that watching the groups already present on the sandy field out of the corner of my eye. For that reason, it was hard for me to imagine someone like Sagor as a mentor.

My face must have appeared like an open book to him, because he guffawed loudly and said, "No, I am your mentor, but I will only practice tactics with you. Fanres will teach you the difficult and rigorous combat techniques. He will be your combat trainer."

Sagor continued to laugh and I was curious what this Fanres would probably look like.

Fanres and the Great Five

We went to the other side of the training grounds to a flat pit in which a boy and a girl were wrestling; both were my age and in leather outfits similar to the one Zaron had worn on my first day in the village.

A dark-haired, well-built man watched them and gave them directions. When he noticed us, he walked over to us laughing.

"Hello, Number Five," he cried with an ironic wink and bowed to Parilar and me.

Questioning, I looked at Sagor who nodded reassuringly.

"Jella, this is your instructor. He is named Fanres and will train you and answer various questions that are naturally rattling around in your head."

"And do you teach both of them also?" I asked Fanres and pointed to the two fighters.

"No, they each have their own mentors and do not belong to the Great Five. I was just giving them tips as I walked by here. Now, come, we'll discuss everything in my hut."

"Many thanks, Sagor," I took leave from my mentor for today.

In Fanres' house, it was cozy and smelled like apples and cinnamon. Not at all fitting for a man of his stature.

Not until now did I have the opportunity to look at him more closely. Fanres was tall, at least six feet two and had wide, muscular shoulders on a massive body. His face was tanned like that of Sagor and finely cut. Under his left eye, three thick scars destroyed his well-proportioned facial expression.

He appeared to have noticed my uncertain look because he clarified without further question, "They come from a battle with a luzo a long time ago. Not all get along with us, among them are also bad-tempered fellows who are not on our side."

Could everyone today read in my face what I was thinking? I decided to behave a little cooler. After all, I was now the number five.

At Fanres' words, Parilar laid his ears back and lowered his eyelids. He looked really angry at this moment. Fanres' comments appeared to upset him.

We had no time for further thought because with a sweeping arm movement, our trainer directed us to take our place.

A large leather-covered sofa stood to the right of the wall, a small brown table out of grained wood stood in front of it. Next to the sofa was a place with blankets for a luzo. Also located in the room were a small fireplace, a dining table and a simple bed. I made out another door on the left side of the back. I suspected that it must lead to the bathroom.

"You can come here anytime, Jella, if something is bothering you or if you have questions. I'm here most of the time anyway, if I am not leading the exercises," began Fanres, making a visible effort to create a pleasant atmosphere.

"Take a seat. Would you like some tea?"

"I would like tea. Do you have black tea?"

"But of course! I have a whole assortment of teas."

That pleased me. A man who collected tea couldn't help but be a likeable representative of his clan.

Parilar lowered himself on the blankets, and I took my place on the soft sofa that turned out to be an uncomfortably hard wooden bench with a leather cover. Fanres returned with the tea and dry cookies and sat down next to me.

"So, now you can get rid of all the questions that are bothering you."

I let loose like shot out of a pistol, "First I have to know what all this here is, what exactly luzos are. And what does it mean 'to be born under Saturn'? And why were our ancestors perhaps wrong? What is my purpose here; what is 'Landuza'? And I don't understand the matter of the 'Great Five' at all. And what will we practice and why and how does one get here and what is the name of the village anyway?"

I would have had another hour worth of further questions to pose in the room, but Fanres, who was just about to drink a sip of tea, waved his hand and interrupted me laughing. In the process, he choked and had to first of all cough.

I took a deep breath and burned my lips in my first attempt sipping from the tea cup.

Fanres continued to laugh and began to tell, "Fine, but one at a time. This here is, so to say, the home of the luzos. There are thousands of them and all are different. Each one looks different, has a different color and each has, like we humans, his own character.

"They are raised by their parents and live in packs in the woods until they can leave their families, where the luzos without riders also live. When they are grown up, those who are suitable are chosen and they are assigned to humans with whom they spend the rest of their lives.

"Originally, all luzos were happy without people in your world. How did it come to this strange symbiosis between cat-like beings and humans? We do not know that any more.

"The time when both came together, the luzos and the people here, lies long ago. The legend tells, however, of a magician who encountered a wounded luzo and healed it. Both became accustomed to one another. The people had driven the magician into banishment, after the land was conquered by foreign intruders who began to drive out or enslave the long-established inhabitants. The magician moved away with the remaining inhabitants and concealed his luzo from the rest of humankind.

"After some time, they discovered a bond between them; that which you today have with Parilar.

"Thanks to our ancestors, who spent most of their time recording everything about these strange and shy creatures, we can recognize who among our people will become riders and prepare them for this from an early age.

"These records of our ancestors are the Codices and are closely guarded. They are our greatest treasure."

Fanres took a brief pause; then he continued, "Luzos are animals that can communicate with us and besides...," he cleared his throat, "...they possess magical powers."

"Magical powers?" I made a doubting face. He didn't want me to believe that there was magic in our world, too. It was slowly becoming too much of a good thing!

"Yes, Jella. But only the luzos and the riders of the Great Five possess them. And they possess them only in unison. Each of them alone cannot activate the magical powers. For that, the bond must exist. Not until the ritual is completed, can the riders access their powers.

"This energy slumbers under the surface and first emerges when it is needed. Some riders never find out what abilities they have because the power was never needed.

"The Great Five stand out above the crowd of luzo riders. They have the responsibility of guarding the Codices of the luzos. Those are scrolls in which our ancestors recorded everything. That is, they are only figuratively scrolls, because they are not made of paper or parchment like the old Egyptians used. They are composed of a material that does not rot, even after thousands of years.

"We do not know what material our ancestors used, but the Codices look today like they always have. And these Codices must be guarded because in them, vital records of the luzos about magic and our village are written down.

"We would be lost if they were ever to disappear. Because there are beings in your world that are ill-disposed toward us. If the Codices were to disappear and they were to find out, we would be in terrible trouble,"

In the meantime, my tea had cooled down somewhat and I took a sip of the warm drink.

"Now to your next question. To be born 'under Saturn' means that one is born into the world in October, November or December.

"Our ancestors named the birth months for the planets that one can see with the naked eye before sunrise: Mercury, Venus, Mars, Jupiter and Saturn. The first two months are assigned to Mercury, the following to Venus. June and July belong to Mars. August and September denote Jupiter and the last three are assigned to Saturn."

Fanres sighed deeply and yawned.

"What else did you want to know?"

My head buzzed; I had to first process all this information before I could think right again. But I gave it my best shot. Only it didn't help much. After another minute, I admitted defeat; I no longer had any questions. My head was empty.

"You wanted to know what 'Landuza' is. And what the name of the village is. And why one cannot find it." Parilar, who had lain still the whole time and listened, intervened with a droning voice.

"Ah, yes, thank you." Fanres was awake again.

"Landuza is the water from the ancient Lake Landuza that provides us with drinking water. From time to time, an underground spring erupts at a particular spot. The water from it has special magical qualities. Our ceremonies are held with it, the traditional rituals, like as an example, your dedication. But only Zaron actually knows about it."

His expression had changed. With a reverently bowed head, he stared into the tea cup in front of him and was silent for a moment.

"Oh, yes, you wanted to know where you are here. Well, listen."

I had been doing that the whole time, why was he so gruff all at once?

"Our village is called Tyrsenor," he said and now with a warm, friendly tone again. So he loved his homeland.

"Here again, we do not know the origin of the name. It is ancient and is probably also mentioned in the codices, but that again is only known by Zaron."

"Is Zaron a kind of high priest?" I interjected.

"Yes and no," replied Fanres.

"He took over the responsibility from his father of keeping the codices and leading the village community. But he is only considered a substitute. According to the legend, the magician who once sealed the first bond with the luzo will someday come again. Until then, an administrator takes over his responsibilities without being endowed with the full powers of the magician."

Our trainer now yawned hard, and I felt worn out from all of the new information. I had stored many more questions in the back of my head, but they simply didn't want to slip into my conscious mind. But then I did have one more question, "And how is this now supposed to continue? What about my life up to now and school; can I still see my friend Rose?"

That was actually three questions at once, but since they slipped out of my mouth in one barrage, one could also let them pass for just one.

"You will go to school like you do every weekday. Only every evening, you are supposed to train with me and Parilar. On the weekends, you will live here and learn and practice with me. I suggest that you come to me one additional day a week so that we can train you more intensively; after all, you have to make up for the lost time when you were unsuspectingly living with the Capuchs. How would it be with Thursday?"

I nodded. That could be arranged. It wouldn't matter to the Capuchs anyway. That would finally bring an end to the cleaning! Just as I was about to make my way home, a last question occurred to me, "Why do the Capuchs want to have nothing to do with the luzos?"

"Some of our people want to lead a completely normal human life and leave us. The Capuch family left us many decades ago, because they did not get along here. At least the children. But they are obligated, to keep everything here...," he made a sweeping gesture, "a secret. You must also keep everything secret."

I sighed in disappointment. I had already guessed as much; I wasn't permitted to tell Rose anything.

The training begins

The next day, after my internship, where I had to sort papers again, Parilar and I flew to Fanres, who wanted to train with us.

On the training grounds, I now met a boy and a girl. Both were tall and wore black leather uniforms with thick shoulder pads that were probably put on for practice.

As we came closer to them they introduced themselves to me.

"Hi! I am Lesla. The number four. Welcome to the Great Five. If you feel like it, we can fly together."

Delighted, I accepted her offer. Lesla's red curls and the little freckles on her button nose were in wonderful harmony with each other. But I especially liked her green eyes. She was friendly to me from the beginning.

The boy appeared to be older than I. His light brown hair and moss green eyes irritated me. Reminded me oddly enough of, of...what?

Yes – of the guy with the brutal eyes that I had seen in my dream and who was threatening the disheveled man who was on his knees in front of him.

Well, not everything resembled him; the boy's eyes were green; those of the man in my dream were yellow. But in spite of that, the two looked incredibly similar.

The boy smiled pleasantly and introduced himself as Lacato, "I am the number one."

I had just enough time to shake his hand before Fanres came over to us and organized the beginning of the exercises.

He explained the course of the next few hours. Lacato and Lesla seemed to be familiar with it; for me, everything was new. Funnily enough, sword fighting and wrestling were part of the training program, as well as flight maneuvers on a luzo's back.

Giggling, I asked Fanres why we were practicing such old-fashioned techniques here in the age of airplanes, cars and computers. Wouldn't every opponent be superior to us with these devices?

He looked at me with daggers that sent a chill up my spine.

"Have you seen a car, plane or computer anywhere here already? That is all folderol from the world in which you lived much too long. Here, all those appliances would be useless metal; no one would be able to use them because we live in a world that has isolated itself from all that."

Whereby I remembered that I still didn't know which country we were in. But I had no time to ask; our trainer drove us mercilessly into the exercises. Lesla and Lacato withdrew; they wanted to practice with their trainer.

Fanres then began with sword fighting. The swords were small and short and forged from a light metal that glistened somewhere between the colors red and green. They were markedly sturdy because when the blades hit one another, there were no nicks at all to be seen. It wasn't steel; all other metals that I knew were also out of the question. Another one of these mystical secrets.

Already after the few minutes in which Fanres just showed me the basic stance and a few simple thrusting techniques, sweat ran down all over me. But my trainer was merciless. We trained two hours without a pause.

He had given me a lighter sword, so he said. To me, it seemed to be a thousand pound sword.

Parilar had watched us and tried to give me tips through our bond, but that confused me so much that the connection between us was finally separated and I could no longer feel him. I was lucky that Lesla and Lacato didn't see me making a fool of myself.

Fanres hit me on the left upper arm with his blunt sword, and I screamed out.

"Ouch, you're crazy!" Quickly, I held my hand in front of my mouth. I had just yelled at my teacher! Could one get a bad grade here for lousy behavior?

"Sorry, I didn't want to..." I stammered horrified.

He interrupted me with a loud laugh, and I looked at him surprised. When he had composed himself, he just said, "You can bad-mouth me as often as you want, if it makes it better for you. Try it like this."

He laid my left hand on the right so that I could use both hands.

"Fight this way first; later when you have learned it better, you will only need to use one hand."

We trained for another two hours. Then I sank to the ground exhausted and wheezed like a fat old walrus. Fanres wasn't even breathing irregularly.

"For starters you have done well. Tomorrow, you will certainly have sore muscles, but try to train with Parilar in spite of that. We'll see one another on Thursday." Fanres bowed to us and we did the same to him.

I was delighted to be able to swing myself onto Parilar's back with the prospect of soon lying in my cozy bed. Even if it was in the Capuchs' house.

"And where will you fly to now?" I asked when Parilar and I arrived in front of the Capuchs' house.

"I will spend the night somewhere in the forest and be with you tomorrow."

Tenderly I let my fingers glide over his fur and felt the warm, hard muscles under his skin. His fur was soft as velvet and already seemed so familiar to me now.

Parilar nudged me encouragingly with his nose and I took another deep breath. Then I turned the key in the door's lock, climbed the steps quietly and lay down in my bed. I didn't make it into the bathroom. The shower could wait until tomorrow morning. Exhausted, I closed my eyes and enjoyed the feeling of being overcome by sleep. I felt calm and I had never experienced such satisfaction. And then the dreams came.

Again, I stood in the junk room and peered through the tiny crack.
Fear crept into me when I looked into the room now. My second I bent sobbing over a disheveled person lying strangely twisted on the floor.
Shivering, I recognized the young man who had been sitting in the chair in the last dream.
Next to him lay the knife that the threatening man had flashed. It was smeared with blood!

Drenched in sweat, I woke up with my heart racing. My whole body was trembling. What did the dream mean? Why did I see myself in a situation that was foreign to me?

Groaning, I sat up and rubbed the sleep out of my eyes. I could rack my brain as much as I wanted; I would not get answers so quickly. But perhaps the nightmares would stop sometime.

It was already becoming light, and so I decided to begin the day with a hot bath. Half asleep, I shuffled into the bathroom and let hot water run into the tub. So far, I didn't feel any sore muscles, but that changed when the warm water enveloped my weary body like an invisible coat.

When I caught sight of my familiar reflection in the mirror, I sensed a feeling of relief. I hadn't changed outwardly – at least that had remained unchanged!

Somehow, the dream had triggered in me the feeling of having aged overnight. I blow-dried my black hair and tied it into a pony tail.

Since the beginning of the week, I had heard nothing more from Rose. She was probably too occupied in the Bengalese Garden. Before the internship, I wanted to quickly see Parilar, so I left the house earlier than usual.

The sun had not yet risen and one could only distinguish the shimmer of a cold dawn on the horizon. Now winter could no longer be stopped; it was already stretching out its greedy fingers and grabbed at everything that looked too fall-like in order to destroy it.

The icy cold stabbed out intensely as I closed the house door behind me. I pulled my cap further down my face right away. If it would at least snow!

The question came to my mind again why I wasn't freezing on the back of the luzo when we flew to the village.

I ran to the edge of the woods and called for Parilar there. I had to repeat my call twice before he finally looked out from behind one of the trees. Laughing, we sauntered into the woods where the ground was covered with fall leaves.

"And how did you survive the night in the dark woods?"

"Oh, quite well, I looked for a cozy spot for myself. I rested and just now hunted a bit..."

I didn't even listen to him anymore; the dream was still weighing on my soul and who other than Parilar could I trust with it?

Unfortunately, I had to interrupt Parilar, because I didn't have much time. No way did I want to arrive late at the police precinct again, and I absolutely wanted to unload my dream beforehand.

"I have to tell you something, Parilar. It has been occupying me for days."

Quickly, I described my dreams to him and my suspicion that it could be about the future. And that Lacato tremendously resembled the threatening man.

53

"I don't believe that it is about the future; if anything, then perhaps about the past, but I am no expert in such matters. I would suggest that you report it to Fanres; he certainly knows more." And with that we headed out.

This evening I stayed up longer than necessary. I was afraid of the dream that could lead me to the shabby room again. Today after the internship I had trained with Parilar for a long time and would have earned a round of sleep, but I tried to keep myself awake with a book. That turned out to be a useless idea, because my eyes were shut already at the first lines. In this night, no nightmares came.

The next morning it poured buckets, and I heard thunder rumbling in the distance. I longed to ride after the storm on Grandma Capuch's old bicycle. But instead of that I dutifully marched to the police precinct.

"Jella, would you like to keep me company a moment with a cup of tea?"

Surprised, I looked at Chief Inspector Terzero who had just called me into his office.

"Of course, gladly!" I answered. With a pot in hand, I made myself comfortable in the red leather chair in Louis' office.

"Is the work fun for you, Jella?" Asked Louis, whom I was permitted to address by his first name in the meantime.

"Um...well yes. As much as filing can be fun," I tried to express myself carefully.

Louis laughed in agreement, "Yes, you're right about that."

We now conversed about all kinds of things and he gave me a little overview of criminalistics by telling me stories of criminals and weaving in something of the methods with which he had run them down.

I found it incredibly thrilling and was pleased that he had taken time to fill me in. Most of all I felt flattered that such an important man as the Chief Inspector cared so much about his interns.

Eventually, he wanted me to tell something about myself and I spoke about my home, how I lived, my stupid sister Camilla, whom I couldn't stand, about Per and Carin and Grandma Drude, avoiding mention of the fact that I was adopted.

And at the very end I rambled on about Rose, talked about her hobby, our flower bed and that she, too, was now doing an internship. And that she always wore a rose in her hair, by which everyone could recognize her from a distance. It did me a world of good to speak to him and we chatted for a while more. In the evening, he insisted upon driving me home.

"Nice cottage," he remarked and thought himself that the word "cottage" was a little understated, because it really didn't do justice to the residence of the Capuchs, which looked more like a villa.

Shortly after dinner, which I ate alone, Parilar waited on the edge of the woods for me and we set off.

During the flight to the village, the same questions assaulted me as in the past days.

Where were we actually flying to? And why wasn't I cold? And what did the dreams mean? The latter occupied me so much that I soon forgot what I wanted to ask Fanres when we arrived.

We only went through a short training since I was much too tired to really work. Afterwards the three of us sat on a stone at the edge of the sandy field.

Now it occurred to me again what I wanted to know the whole time: In what region were we here actually? I was good in geography at school. After the takeoff, Parilar always turned to the east so that by my estimation we should at some point see Drammen or even Oslo already appear.

But nothing of the sort happened. After a short time, we always came into a belt of fog and the unfamiliar mountains appeared in front of us. To be sure, the flight time was too short for us to have been able to leave Norway behind us. And this is what I now asked Fanres, "Where are we here?"

He looked at me from the side and said, "In Tyrsenor, you know that."

"No, that's not what I meant. In which region are we here? I know enough about geography to judge that this here is not Norway," I said with a somewhat haughty tone.

Fanres laughed and then looked at Parilar.

"That is actually a secret, Miss Know-It-All."

With that, he probably wanted to make it clear that I didn't have to show off here.

"Well then, I will try to explain it to you. But it is complicated and I also didn't comprehend everything," he then continued.

My luzo also listened eagerly, his pointed ears raised. Didn't he know all about it?

"When Parilar brings you to us, he flies into a wall of fog. In reality, that is an energy field that only a special group of luzos can generate. Only very few are endowed with this gift and these are the ones who help us to survive. The details probably are in one of the books of the codices, but only Zaron has access to them and therefore you would have to ask him about it."

Meanwhile it had become clear to me that a conversation with Zaron would be about as easy to get as an audience with King Harald of Norway. So I could cross that off.

Now Fanres began further explanations:

"In the energy field that the luzos construct it can come to an extreme compression of the space-time structure for a short time. Please don't ask me what that is; I have only overheard it in conversations in the Council of the Eldest after the Capuch family left us and we discussed how that would go. They had doubtless found that out.

"In this compression, something like a hole in time forms itself that certain luzos can slip through. You are not in just another place here; you are also in another time."

Now I was so stunned that my mouth remained open. To be honest, I understood nothing and already believed myself to be the object of a bad joke.

Until I recalled the physics class at school in which Mr. Bergenson told us a few months ago about a theory, that he called the "Theory of Relativity." Physics was something he was versed in. Every time he chattered about it, he appeared to change and perked up thoroughly. He had almost no idea about the rest of the sciences or anything else and we felt those things also bored him.

Now it occurred to me that he once said that space and time are actually the same and that they belong together inseparably.

So one would have to, he said, if one can move in space, that is from place to place, also be able to move back and forth in time. Back then he also said, however, that a certain Mr. Einstein had calculated that was only possible in a - what was that complicated word again? - *space-time singularity*, for which one would have to concentrate a huge amount of energy on one point.

And this point would be unique and therefore one named it *singularity*. Because 'singular' means one. And that would be technically impossible; there was no material that would withstand that.

I incorporated this complicated word zealously to prove to Fanres that I knew a lot. Continuing to be the "know it all."

"Fanres," I asked, "does that mean that Parilar has the ability to form a *space-time singularity* around him? And with that to produce a tunnel between different times?"

The sentence slid out of my lips like oil and I was proud to be able to state something so complicated without stuttering. I didn't know myself what that could mean, but felt vaguely that this would describe the situation.

Fanres looked at me with a face that showed at the same time amazement and annoyance.

"Yes, thunderation, how do you know all that?' he blustered. Apparently he was embarrassed to have a student who was superior to him in some areas.

"Well that's exactly the word that I once heard from Hakan Capuch's father, that is, Per's grandfather, before they moved away," he muttered to himself.

Grumbling, he continued, "I wouldn't have been able to express it like that, but he used that word. We are in another time here, in another timeframe so to say, and we are the only people with the ways and means to move forwards and backwards in it. That is, only sometimes one or sometimes two luzos can do that, but don't ask me why."

Now my curiosity was really awakened.

"We are here in another time than that which, for example, is to be seen on the clocks in Drammen?" I asked breathlessly.

This was getting more and more thrilling! For a student who was one of the few in class to be interested in natural sciences, this was grist in my mill.

"And what time is it now?" I asked full of enthusiasm.

Fanres looked at Parilar. He had closed his eyes and didn't make a sound. When I tried to ask him through our bond, something weird happened, that I had never before experienced with him.

The cat slowly opened its eyes. Under them the pupils suddenly shone green and emitted a strangely surreal light that illuminated the space in front of us in evening light. And then I perceived a voice unfamiliar to me

57

over the invisible bond that held us together. The voice was rough and sounded as if it were speaking to us out of a deep cavern.

"That is a secret that you will confide to no one. That which I share with you will remain hidden in you. Only when the time has come to use the secret knowledge for the good of Tyrsenor are you permitted to reveal it. Go back two thousand years in your measurement of time. Then you will arrive here."

The voice fell silent. Parilar closed his eyes again. I sat as if petrified between Fanres and the luzo. Shock sat deep in my limbs: That wasn't Parilar who had spoken to me?

Fanres looked at me and said in a quiet voice, "Now you are probably the only person far and wide to know the secret and know where we live."

The sun had gone down and I still couldn't move; what I had heard stirred me so deeply.

It was slowly becoming clear to me that I was moving between two different worlds.

Parilar was awake again and now looked at me questioningly. I was now sure that he knew nothing of what had just happened. And so, with a dull voice, I asked him to take me back. Back to a time that was yet to come.

At home, I fell onto my pillow exhausted. I could feel every one of my bones. Perhaps it would be better to not always know everything that was happening? I trembled myself slowly into a restless sleep.

Vacation

This time I found MYSELF not in the shabby room again, but in a huge room, that was lit after a fashion by some flickering candles.
Again I saw my second "I". She hastily gathered papers together that looked as if they had been forged out of metal, thin and glossy.

In the course of this, my "I" kept looking hurriedly at the door and sobbed loudly and unrestrained. Apparently "I" was sad and extremely frightened. Finally, the dream-Jella ran with the papers in her arms to a wall, on which a huge portrait of a luzo hung.

Carefully "I" pushed the picture aside. A secret passageway became visible. My dream-I slipped through the hiding spot and pushed the picture in front of the opening again.

As if numb, I myself remained back in the room and stared at the open drawer, on which an ornate script was visible:
"βιβλίον πρωτεῖον ‖ Codex Pars Primum"

The moon shone palely into my room when I awakened this night. It was the third night on which this type of dream had haunted me. "I" had stolen the first part of the Codices in the dream. I wouldn't be able to bear this much longer.

These dreams were wearing on my nerves. I took a glass of milk from the kitchen and sat down in the living room. Outside, the wind whistled around our house and I listened to it until my eyes fell shut.

"Damn it, why are you sleeping here. Aren't you supposed to be at police headquarters?"

Half-asleep, I squinted into the angry face of Per, who had rudely shaken me awake. Rats, I had fallen asleep on the living room sofa.

"What time is it?" I inquired while I sat up.

"Late enough. And now quickly, get yourself moving."

I sleepily took care of the breakfast table, made coffee and crept out of the house with aching limbs.

On the last day of the internship I was permitted to go along with Louis on a routine patrol through the city, during which we warned a few youths not to spray graffiti on the walls of houses and collected the identification of a drunk. Finally we drove the intoxicated man home, who during the drive bellowed "Old MacDonald had a farm" without pause.

After this, began first of all a few days of vacation, which were added in extra this year. On the last day of the internship I had, in addition, decided in an attack of cockiness to just skip school in the future.

At least for a few weeks until the next interim examination.

I simply had no desire, on the one hand, to do the practices in Tyrsenor and then to sit dutifully in school the next day and act as if there had been nothing. A few weeks of classes more or less, what difference would it make? The material for the final examination was already in my head anyway.

But for that I would need Per. He would have to excuse me, otherwise he would get aggravation from the school authorities and everything could be blown. When that suddenly became clear to me, I let my head hang in disappointment. But then in the evening I mustered up all of my courage and told him in an attack of spitefulness what I wanted.

To my surprise he didn't simply say no, but just acknowledged my suggestion with a reluctant grunt. He would excuse me from school. The main thing would be that I would leave him in peace.

I was so perplexed that I didn't ask any further. Otherwise he would back down in the end! Or worse yet: ask Carin! Yuck!

Now I looked forward to the weekend when I would really recover from the internship.

On this Saturday morning, I first went to Grandma and Grandpa Capuch. I had completely forgotten them the Wednesday before and now I missed them. So many incredible things had happened that I no longer found time for the normal things in life,

"Hi! Hakan!" I greeted Grandpa Capuch.

"Oh, hi, Jella. Nice that you are here. Drude is just baking an apple cake. Would you like to eat it with or without whipped cream?"

I grinned; I loved these hours with Drude and Hakan.

"With, please."

After Drude had planted a wet kiss on my cheek, we enjoyed the delicious apple cake."

"Jella, Jella!"

I turned to Hakan. "What's wrong?"

"Nothing. What would be wrong?" Questioningly, he looked at me out of his old eyes.

"Didn't you just call me?"

Hakan furrowed his wrinkled forehead.

"I'm not so old that I forget what I have said."

I was about to disagree with a "but" when I heard the calls again and became abruptly aware of who was calling me: Parilar! In my thoughts I shot back, "What's up? I'm with Grandma and Grandpa Capuch."

"I'm happy for you, but have you forgotten that we train on weekends?"

I inhaled air sharply.

"Yes, I did. Pick me up immediately. I'm coming!"

Turning to Drude and Hakan I said, "I'm sorry; I need to go take care of something urgent."

And was out of the house; the dumbfounded faces of Drude and Hakan looked after me aghast. I heard Parilar fly up and already, I sat on his back!

Fanres was already waiting for us with a scowling face about our lateness and we immediately began with battle training.

In the next weeks we continued that, beginning immediately and without interruption. We completed our training in three disciplines: first was sword-fighting with which I spent the first week. With astonishingly light and yet almost indestructible short swords we practiced feints, strokes, cuts, evasion and subterfuge and the corresponding steps.

I didn't like wrestling so much, but I did well in this subject after some time. In doing so, it was less about strength-emphasized wrestling than learning holds and evasive maneuvers with which one could leverage and conquer a physically stronger opponent.

The exercises in this discipline reminded me a little of judo, but they were less physical and I hardly needed strength to employ the tricks and holds that Fanres and later Sagor showed me.

I liked the flight exercises with my luzo the best. We practiced the greatest air maneuvers over the grounds, turning out of a fast flight, quick curved flight, stopping short in the air and then dropping, rolling and much more.

The only thing that I couldn't stand was loop-the-looping. In doing this, I panicked every time, which initially tempted Parilar to play jokes on me until we once got into a fight and I screamed at him after a daredevil loop.

According to Fanres, we had only little time to make up the lag behind the other members of the Great Five. Inside of few weeks I had to learn what the other four had been practicing for many years. Therefore he tried to practice with me in such a way that I was in the position to quickly bridge my physical deficit and improve my skill at a fast pace.

That didn't function the way he envisioned, however. After all, the other four had studied their skills for several years already and built up corresponding mental and physical capabilities.

It was foreseeable with me, Fanres said, that in spite of the excellent qualifications that I brought with me, it would not be possible to make up for the training deficit in a reasonable time frame.

Fanres and Sagor decided therefore to focus on tactics and tricks. I was extraordinarily agile and as adroit as a squirrel, Parilar once commented and one could build upon that. The effect was astonishing. Within a few days I already learned tricks with which I could take out considerably stronger men than myself and I made an enormous leap ahead in my adroitness.

In sword fighting, I only succeeded one out of every hundred times in setting the practice sword on Fanres' chest. The other ninety-nine times it ended the other way around. Because of this I took more time for the exercises that required keen attention and ruses, but not strength. Kickboxing also went along with that, primarily techniques to avoid one's opponent and use his own strength against him.

In spite of his corpulence, Sagor, who after some time took over this part of the training, was amazingly adept at these techniques. He showed me how I could double-cross even the biggest fighter in spite of my physical weakness.

I developed an extraordinary respect for him. I had never seen an adroitness of this kind in a man of his stature! And best of all: He proved to be an excellent teacher who explained everything to me so well and led me in a way that almost everything sank in instantly.

However, my favorite remained the flight exercises with my luzo. For that, one needed instinct. And with Parilar, I could not only practice in the village but also on the way back and forth and in the dark, often over the Egerskogen; we made a game of thinking up the craziest exercises. Except for loop-the-looping goes without saying. Sometimes Parilar and I demonstrated how we had trained and raked in much praise for ourselves.

Oddly enough all of the five practiced separately from one another, every pair with its own trainer and I could only now and then watch other luzos doing flight maneuvers at a distance.

Glimpse into a distant time

Several weeks passed this way, practicing exhaustively and having fun.

On one of the practice days, Fanres came toward us after an extensive fight lesson, "You're making excellent progress, Jella. You have made up almost the entire training deficit. Now we can bring you together with the others. You and the other four will practice together and with other luzos. Now, come, we will indulge ourselves in a cup of tea." He winked at me.

"Then you will be dismissed for the day."

The nightmares from the beginning of the late fall still weighed heavily on my mind; I had experienced them repeatedly in the past few weeks and couldn't forget them. I desperately wanted to speak to someone about them. Now I saw the chance to tell Fanres about my dreams.

In his hut, I then approached him while he was putting the water for the tea over the fire.

"Fanres, I have a question. One that is preying on my mind. I have..."

I faltered. Now the question seemed ridiculous. Everyone had bad dreams now and then. I decided to let it be.

"Feel free to ask; you can trust me with anything," he said with a gentle voice.

"Oh, nothing important. I wanted to just...just hear more about the Great Five." Which was also not a lie!

Fanres came with two steaming cups of tea and sat on the stool across from me.

"Well, there is a lot to hear. I'll simply tell you the most important things.

"The Great Five possess, as you already know, special powers. They have received these so that they can protect our village and its secrets.

"Since a long, long time ago, a new group of riders is formed in every generation. You are the most recent fighters in the long tradition.

"The generation before yours consisted of two female and three male riders. They were named Beleia, Catleya, Lacanias, Adrian und Gribor. The three most important were probably Catleya, Adrian and Gribor.

"Catleya possessed the talent to control dreams or send dreams to the sleeping. Along with that came also the ability to sometimes read dreams, even if a person was far away from her. She just needed to concentrate hard;

then she learned a lot. But she was a good person and dealt with this talent diligently and carefully.

"Adrian had a big heart and the gift of transforming material things. For example, an iron ring into a scrap of cloth. The ring would then remain a piece of cloth until it was sprinkled with a few drops of Landuza water. Then the original took on its true form again.

"Beleia was a healer and seer, who was blessed with special magical powers and stood in contact with other worlds. She helped us when we needed to fetch things from your world or bring them there. She could move small pieces of matter between the worlds or materialize a thing here which we needed.

"We never learned what the magic abilities of Lacanias were; he disappeared one day in a mysterious manner after the last group of the Great Five was dissolved, which I'll now tell you about.

"Gribor was an ambitious, militant man who backed away from nothing. It was his gift to be able to make himself invisible for a period of time and so be able to appear everywhere unseen.

"Catleya and Adrian felt a deep attraction for one another and fell in love. That was the first time in many generations that two of the Great Five got together. Well, the story began very happily. Together the Great Five had grand days until suddenly the first part of the Codices disappeared."

At these words, a chill ran up my spine.

"No one knew why, but Gribor accused Catleya and Adrian of having committed the theft. Because they had had the task of standing guard over the Codices on this evening.

"Then everything went quite fast. Adrian was found stabbed to death in his house and Catleya disappeared. Gribor, so one says, went into hiding the same evening and he left his wife and his small son Lacato behind. He was probably distraught about the crime that Adrian had committed."

Lacato. Did he just say "Lacato"?

"THE Lacato?"

Fanres nodded his head momentously.

"Lacato is in fact Gribor's son," he confirmed.

I was speechless. That all fit together so well with my dreams.

When the light suddenly went on for me, I had to swallow hard. The murder, the theft. That was not my second I. And Adrian was...

"Fanres, is there still a picture of the three?" I asked quite excited.

He hesitated and watched me with an uncertain look, but affirmed, "Sagor will surely be able to track down pictures somewhere. He had them painted in his time. Would you like to right away or..."

I nodded vigorously and jumped up. Fanres threw a further questioning look my way, however, didn't reply.

We found Sagor in his workroom, where he was sorting some papers. The ceiling height of the room corresponded to his body size and Fanres was forced to bend himself under the low black ceiling beams so that he didn't hit his head.

"A badger's burrow, this..." he growled grimly when he did hit once.

Sagor ignored his ranting and smiled at us mischievously, "Oh, what a pleasure! What brings you here?"

I asked him outright for the pictures and he at once supplied me with a choice of small paintings. The individuals were depicted so exactly that one could have mistaken the portraits for photographs.

I became white as a sheet when I saw them. My knees shook and I had to hold onto the table. Why hadn't it occurred to me earlier?

"Jella, is everything OK?" Fanres concerned voice pulled me out of my state of shock.

"I don't know, I...may I take that along?" I stuttered.

Sagor nodded and looked at me, dismayed.

"You look terrible; I hope you're not getting sick. Just go; Parilar will take you home."

I could still hear Sagor saying "Get well!" to me in parting when Fanres had already pushed me outside.

In this moment a creature with red curls came toward us and grasped the situation at once.

"Oh, God, should I accompany you home?" Lesla asked genuinely concerned. I smiled gratefully until occurred to me that Fanres wanted to do that.

"That's all right. I have something else to take care of anyway. So long!" With these words, Fanres hurried to his hut.

"Is that the generation before us?" Lesla asked interested.

I still had the picture of the last group of the Great Five in my hand. Dazed, I nodded.

"Wow, I've already heard so much about them; They were very powerful. This one here-," she pointed to the attractive face with the light eyes framed with light brown curls. "Gribor. That is Lacato's father. Corey is namely his half-brother..."

"Corey is Lacato's brother? I gasped.

Lesla answered with a nod.

It was all becoming weirder and weirder.

Parilar and a greenish colored luzo stood side by side when we arrived.

"That's Jali," Lesla introduced me to her luzo.

She climbed on Jali's back; I hopped on Parilar, probably a little too hard because he winced, and both of us flew away.

A first clue

Lesla had accompanied me up to the wall of fog. Together we flew through the early evening. It was unbelievably beautiful!

I forgot my scare almost immediately. Just before the cloud of energy, Lesla had to turn around; it wasn't possible for Jali to form the same field as Parilar. Flying together was much more fun and Lesla was an adorable person. For that reason, I would have liked to take her along, but she couldn't go through the barrier. I had taken my new friend into my heart right away.

Just like Rose in her time. I had to suddenly swallow when a sad feeling came over me.

Rose. I hadn't heard anything from her in so long.

Actually, that is, I had neglected her because I was too occupied with my adventures and my new friends.

"That's not how you treat your best friend," I scolded myself in my thoughts and decided to visit Rose as soon as possible.

After we had landed in Hokksund, I said goodbye to Parilar and promised to tell him the next morning what was bothering me. Then I disappeared into bed with a hot water bottle at once. I slept with the painting in my hand and...

...found myself in the forest again. A gentle breeze enveloped me and carried me through the canopy of deciduous leaves. I floated over the tips of the Egerskogen and felt weightless. The weightlessness suddenly abated and I felt gravity again. Panic-stricken I fell and fell until I landed hard on the floor of the forest. My muscles burned from the impact, yet no cry of pain escaped my lips because I strained to listen. Did I actually hear the beating of wings?

I was right; a huge luzo broke through the canopy of leaves. The sun flattered the golden fur of the animal and blinded me so that I couldn't recognize the rider who suddenly threw a fine necklace at my feet. The chain was out of pure gold and on it hung a small circular pendant that gleamed like silver. When I looked up again, the huge golden luzo had disappeared. Nothing remained behind. Only the chain lay coolly in my hands.

I awoke. My bones hurt; it felt like huge drums were banging in my head.

Suddenly I cringed. Something hard was pressing gently on my cheek. Half-asleep I felt around for it and tore open my eyes in astonishment.

The gold chain from my dreams dangled from my neck and had gotten pushed sideways under my cheek as I slept, leaving an indentation behind.

Why was it hanging on my neck? And how could I have gotten it here from my dream?

Or perhaps Per had placed it on my pillow as a sign of apology for his rudeness and had unconsciously slipped it on yesterday? That would be a pleasant surprise; perhaps the Capuchs were changing their attitude?

"Dream on," I then thought in resignation. "Certainly not them."

But then who had left the little necklace on the pillow? Rose?

Naturally, who else! She probably was here yesterday and wanted to remind me of our friendship with the necklace. But where would Rose scrape up so much money for gold jewelry? And then give it to me as well? I bit my lip; my guilty conscience now plagued me and threw my thoughts out of kilter.

Confused, I looked at the clock. It was still long before daybreak and I decided to go to Parilar on the edge of the woods once again and explain my behavior yesterday.

I didn't need to call him for long. He came flying hastily and landed elegantly next to me in front of the house. Everyone was sleeping which made our meeting easier. Together we went a ways into the woods.

"Yesterday I discovered something. I myself was surprised, I had no idea..." I began.

"Yeah, yeah, cut the long story short. What's so urgent that you summoned me here in the middle of the night?" he hissed. Apparently he in a bad mood. Perhaps I was keeping him from the hunt, and he had been forced to let a wild boar go that was supposed to be his breakfast. Well, that could wait.

"Okay. Well, I believe I now know who my parents were! Here."

I showed him the small portrait painting. I hadn't seen myself in my dreams; but instead my mother. And the disheveled man was my father. I had recognized him because he had the same icy blue eyes as I did.

Stunned, Parilar stared at the picture.

"They really look markedly similar to you, but that cannot be possible. They disappeared an eternity ago." He didn't get any further.

"Parilar, I can surely recognize my own parents!"

Even Parilar had no answer to that. Now I described my crazy dream to him and showed him the necklace with the silver pendant. Baffled, he examined it.

"Don't tell Fanres anything about this strange dream and the pendant. Let's wait a bit; perhaps we will find an explanation for everything..." he said to my astonishment.

Here was a clue to my parents! My greatest longing to find out my destiny and that of my parents appeared possible to fulfill! And then this luzo put on the brakes and didn't want me to devote of my energy to finding out what had happened back then! Inwardly, I protested fiercely and was torn back and forth in my storm of feelings.

But something in my gut told me that Parilar was right. I had to be careful. The dreams were about a crime. The codices had been stolen. Had it been my mother? And hadn't a murder occurred as well? Could I trust my parents at all after what Fanres had told me? What if my mother had disappeared with Gribor and both had taken the codices with them?

My head was spinning again.

Too many questions, too many uncertainties. I had to go about this carefully. Parilar and I parted from one another and I went back into the house to begin the day's work.

Today I was going to school again. My guilty conscience and my feeling of longing to see Rose led me to end my self-imposed extended vacation. I wanted to see my best friend again.

Oddly enough, no one at school seemed to have really missed me, because they all greeted me as if I were recovered after a long illness.

"How are you? Did you make a good recovery? Nice to see you back on your feet." And so forth.

Per had done excellent work with his excuses and apologies. I just murmured something vague and acted as if it had been nothing.

Then I waited for Rose, who I would have liked to greet with an exuberant hug and ask about the meaning of the necklace and her experiences. But she didn't come and I wondered sadly if she had stayed home sick.

I missed her; it would have been good to listen to her voice and tales and laughter after all the weeks of separation even though I couldn't confide anything about my worries in her. But the memory of her laugh alone improved my worried mood and soon I had forgotten the dreams for now.

After the bell at the end of the school day, I took leave of my other classmates. Secretively I crept directly to the woods without going home first and called for Parilar. We left without delay for Tyrsenor, where I hoped to become enlightened about the fate of my parents.

The Great Five

"I wanted to ask you if you want to fly with Lacato and me." Lesla stood on the outskirts of the village' apparently she had been waiting for us.

I quickly looked around. Lacato was nowhere in sight! I hesitated, but finally gave in. "Yes, why not? Where is he?"

"He's sitting at home unaware of his good luck."

But we took this path in vain because Lacato was already at the training grounds and practicing with his luzo. When he noticed us, he interrupted his practice.

"Do you want to come along for a short spin?" Lesla patted Lacato's luzo on the neck. In doing that, she looked at him from the side so that I noticed that she downright worshipped him! Was she in love with him?

Number one agreed with pleasure. He appeared to like the idea of taking off with us...

Today was the first time that all of us were permitted to fly together. It felt as if school was over and we had been permitted to enjoy our freedom. The nightmares were forgotten and I wanted to enjoy a magnificent day. The three of us flew across the sky although it had begun to spit.

As if out of nowhere, a fourth rider on a reddish brown luzo appeared all of a sudden. I looked at him startled, and the young rider had to laugh at my expression.

He was not much younger than I, had flax-colored blond hair and daring eyes that flashed in amusement.

"I am Fedor the number four!" he shouted over to me through the rushing wind, laughing. He had to repeat that twice until I had finally understood.

And now another girl with brown hair and blue eyes whooshed by laughing and introduced herself as Lauren, the number three. Now I was familiar with all of the Great Five after only having met Lacato and Lesla up to now:

Number One: Lacato, at the same time the eldest.
Number Two: Lesla, the playful one.
Number Three: Lauren, the laughing one.
Number four: Fedor, the daredevil
Number five: Jella, I myself, the dreamy one.

And I was damned proud of that!

The gentle drizzle had turned into a strong downpour, but now it was even so much more fun that we circled around one another and then flew apart again. Not until evening did we sail toward the ground.

Now it was raining in buckets and we were soaked to the skin. In spite of the fall weather, I was still not freezing and my new friends also displayed no sign of hypothermia. The energy emanating from the luzos appeared to transfer to us and keep the cold away.

"Come, we can warm up at my place," suggested Lacato nevertheless. So, apparently someone else was freezing. But after I had dismounted, I also noticed how the wet clothes were conducting the heat out of my body. The energy of the luzos had earlier surrounded us so that the rain couldn't touch us. But now the cool precipitation could soak up our warmth. But the temperature was still much more pleasant than at home in Hokksund.

Our luzos disappeared into a nearby cave and we followed Lacato into his hut. It was furnished exactly like my own room in this village, which I had been permitted to use for a few weeks now. Only it seemed more lived-in.

He gave each of us a blanket and we took off our pants and sweaters to place them over the stove to dry. With a steaming cup of tea in our hands we then soon snuggled together.

It felt great to do something with friends. Until now, I had only had one friend who was as close to me as these four were now. That was Rose. At this moment, I had to admit that I missed her as much as my parents. At the instant when I thought of her, a small tear pushed its way into the corner of my eye. But no one had seen it.

Yet this here, the togetherness with my new friends felt great.

"Aren't your adoptive parents worried?" Lesla looked at me curiously.

I shook my head. "They only worry about their daughter Camilla." I told her about my former life and how I had to clean and straighten up for the Capuchs, that they treated me like a servant, and my interests came last. If there could even be any talk of my interests. Well, nonetheless, I could attend school and Per made sure that I had time for the luzos. But the Capuchs could not replace my parents. And apparently they didn't want to either.

It did me good to be able to express myself and let everything out. We talked the whole time until the full moon now showed high in the cloudless sky again and laughed with another. One after another, everyone but me fell asleep.

I couldn't sleep yet. Lost in thought I played with the pendant and asked myself what it could mean. Or did it have any meaning at all? When I could no longer stand it among all of the sleeping, I carefully stood up, taking care to not awaken anyone.

Lesla had laid her head on my knee in her sleep. Carefully I lifted it and stuffed a pillow under her head.

Suddenly I heard her whisper, "Where are you going?" She raised her head, half-asleep.

"I wanted to check on Parilar. Go back to sleep."

But she got up rubbing her eyes and said, "I'll come along. It's too stuffy for me here."

We grabbed our clothes and together, we found our luzos snuggled together in the cave.

"Parilar, are you still awake?"

An annoyed grumbling was audible. His mood really appeared not to be the best today. Well, that's how cats are, moody, dependent on atmosphere... I couldn't suppress a grin.

Lesla had already nestled alongside of her luzo. For my part, I leaned myself against Parilar, who good-naturedly made his warm belly available. He lowered one wing so that he enveloped me protectively.

"What's it actually like when one goes to school? Lesla asked me with a quiet voice.

"Well, sometimes it gets on your nerves, but basically I can't complain," I answered.

"It's nice to be together with others and most of the time it's even fun to learn new things. Especially in classes about science. And you really don't go to school?" It was hard for me to imagine; everyone needed to go to school for at least a few years!

"I don't go to a school. I learn reading, writing and some crafts here for three hours in the morning and arithmetic once a week. It wouldn't be enough to not embarrass myself on a visit to your world, but none of us gets

74

there anyway. In the present generation they say only your luzo has the ability to leave our land."

"And you're satisfied with that?"

"Hmmm..." Lesla thought it over.

"I would like to go to a school sometime. And see how everything works there..."

"Then just come along with me once!" I suggested enthusiastically. "Parilar can surely carry both of us."

"Who do you believe they would think I was? They would at most make fun of me."

At that, nothing else occurred to me and soon I fell into a deep sleep.

The morning sun illuminated the cave with a golden glow. When I stretched, I felt an unpleasant pain in my back. That had come from the uncomfortable place to sleep.

Lesla still slept at the side of Jali who greeted me joyfully. I petted Jali's nose and briefly scratched her behind the ear.

"Great, I don't get a good morning greeting, do I?" Parilar stalked out of the cave insulted. Well, whatever was eating him yesterday was apparently still bugging him.

Laughing, I followed him and playfully punched him on his side. "Come on, you old grouchy cat," I teased him. "School is waiting for me."

The ankle cuff

Rose was again not in her place when I went into the school. She didn't appear the whole morning; surely she was really sick, not just out of sorts. I began to worry about her and planned once more to visit her soon. But the training and above all my new friends were more important to me at the present time.

Later after school. Parilar and I flew to Tyrsenor where only ground exercises were on the agenda. Parilar set off with a group of luzos to, as they said, train together with them. I rather believed that they wanted to go hunting because their flashing eyes expressed their excitement and the tips of their tails twitched to and fro. Probably they had smelled wild boars, their favorite meal.

Fanres and I went to the training field, where I found Lauren, who was conducting a sword fight with her mentor. Her brunette hair swirled like a dark waterfall and she moved with such elegance that my jaw dropped open in astonishment.

"Soon you will be able to do exactly the same, " Fanres tried to encourage me and laid his hand on my shoulder,

"Yes, of course," I added doubtfully and got started. With a hard stroke, my blade crashed into Fanres' armored shoulder causing him to pause dumbfounded. My chance! Effortlessly I spun around him and placed my sword on his chest. I laughed triumphantly. And now he laughed also. I was proud of my first victory.

Fanres, Sagor and I continued to practice until early evening. I had Parilar, who now was in an extraordinarily good mood, take me home.

Back at home in my room at the Capuchs', I took off my shoes, when I noticed something black around my ankle. I observed it more closely and realized distressed that it was the electronic ankle cuff of Louis!

What was it doing here and how did it get around my ankle? How in the world did it get on my ankle unnoticed? I no longer understood the world; what was this supposed to be? Panic rose up my back and the muscles in my neck cramped up.

Fiercely I pulled and wrenched at the band, but I simply couldn't get it off. I ran out of the house without shoes and yelled inwardly for Parilar. I was filled with fear and could no longer suppress the feeling of being threatened by something inexplicable. Something which was there but which I couldn't comprehend. Like a spirit, something that watched me, that unsettled me to the core.

"Parilar? Can you help me? I can't get this thing off of my foot!" I whimpered in fear. He was already at our customary meeting place at the edge of the woods when I arrived. With a quiet "crack" he removed the band from me with his teeth.

"What is that?" He curiously examined the band.

"An electronic ankle cuff. I recognize it from my police internship. I don't have the foggiest notion how it could have gotten onto my foot," I gasped.

Parilar shrugged his shoulders. "Some things get legs or you yourself forget what you did with it," he said carefully.

"You think I wouldn't remember pocketing the electronic ankle bracelet and fastening it around my foot?" I asked indignantly.

"Could be...?"

I tapped my forehead. He didn't believe that himself. The incident continued to greatly upset me because if I hadn't fastened the black thing around my ankle, then it must have been someone else. I was too exhausted, however, to be able to bring my thoughts to a conclusion.

Tomorrow Fanres would fly with me to Lake Landuza; he had promised me that. Only a few chosen ones were permitted to visit this lake and I was among those who were chosen for this.

Then I would ask him and request that he explain what he thought of all this. The dreams, the ankle cuff and...

Especially one thing I wanted to know from him: Had he ever heard anything from my mother again? Was she perhaps still alive?

While I thought about that, hot and cold shivers ran over my back and my heart beat in my throat.

The police return

Back at home a police car stood in front of the villa.

I was surprised. Did Chief Inspector Louis want to visit me? Or did it have something to do with the ankle cuff that Parilar had just torn? Somehow I felt uneasy; had I done something wrong?

In my thoughts, I again went through all the conversations Louis and I had had during my week's internship. Nothing occurred to me that I could have overlooked or forgotten. But my guilty conscience remained.

Hesitantly, I opened the door and crept through the hallway toward the stairs when Per saw me and called after me. He sat at his work table with two uniformed officials, an older sergeant and a young woman whose rank was inspector, as I was able to note from the emblems on her sleeves, and a cup of tea stood before them.

"Come in and close the door," Per snapped at me.

Both officials rose when I entered, intimidated. They came toward me and greeted me with a friendly handshake. So it couldn't be all that bad.

In spite of that, my brain rattled like crazy and tried to figure out what I had done wrong. But only the ankle cuff came to mind. If it was registered as stolen and they had found out that I had it? How could I make clear to them that I couldn't remember it at all?

"Hello, Jella. I am Inspector Laura Turgel," said the young policewoman kindly, but with an accent that made me flinch. Was she an American? But she wore a Norwegian uniform. She was short and wiry and the short bristly hair on her narrow head over her pointed upturned nose made me think of a hedgehog. The cold blue eyes with which she scrutinized me from head to toe were to be feared. Then she smiled and I was relieved.

"And this is Sergeant Oliver Johns," she introduced her older colleague, who was at least a head taller and probably surpassed his colleague with at least two times her waist size. More like three times. From school, I knew of a village in Ireland with the same name and judging from the facial expression of Sergeant Johns, he had already frequently formed a friendship with the whiskey of the island.

78

Bright red cheeks were streaked with dark blue capillaries; his bulbous nose must surely serve him well finding the way home at night, because it glowed like a red flashlight.

For a brief moment, I forgot my fear of the strange duo and had to suppress a giggle. But probably he was named "Johanson" and not "Johns" and his colleague had omitted the last syllable with her accent.

"Jella," Inspector Turgel interrupted my musings, "We are from the Missing Persons Bureau, the department for missing people in Drammen and are here on account of Katharina Barbara Hamson. She is missing. Have you heard something from her?"

I became pale, my knees began to shake, and now my thoughts really began to race. Katharina Hamson was the real name of my best friend Rose and I hadn't seen her for several days now. After my internship, I hadn't had time to visit her because of my training.

And so in my concentration on Parilar and my village, I hadn't even noticed that Rose hadn't appeared already for quite a few days (or even weeks?).

Somehow I must have felt that something wasn't right because my guilty feelings now flooded me with reproach. How could I simply lose sight of my best friend? Why hadn't it occurred to me that she was staying away? And why the devil hadn't I contacted her? ' And...and...and...

"Are you not well?" the policewoman interrupted my stream of thoughts. It occurred to me that I had not yet spoken the whole time. Only a few moments had passed since my entrance, but in this short time, my whole world had collapsed. Rose was missing and I felt miserable.

"Since when has she been missing?" I asked with a squeaky voice, completely intimidated.

"Officially since three weeks ago, but apparently she hasn't been seen since the Friday of the week before last" the fat sergeant now started in. His voice really sounded like an empty whiskey barrel.

"Now, pull yourself together" a thought shot through my head. "Rose is missing and you are kidding around here," my conscience scolded me.

"She told her mother the week before last that she wanted to visit a girlfriend whom she had met during her internship for the weekend in Oslo.

She gave the name Ariana Bankshire. Allegedly she had come into the country as an exchange student. Do you know the girl?"

I shook my head. "I have never heard the name. I didn't even know that Rose had met someone during her internship."

"Who is Rose?" the policewoman interrupted me.

"I meant Katharina; for me, she is named Rose because she always wears a rose in her hair," I answered.

"Aha, that's her nickname," said the sergeant.

His colleague looked at him wryly from the side, "Such a thing is not a nickname. Girlfriends give themselves friendly names and don't tease one another like boys," she corrected him.

Then she turned back to me, "Tell us when you last saw her. And what you talked about together the last time."

I turned red and lowered my head. Now I had to admit that I hadn't concerned myself with my best friend in the past few weeks.

"I believe that we last spoke with one another before the internship," I said with a quiet voice.

"Speak louder," the fat sergeant snapped at me.

"Keep your trap shut," the lean policewoman abruptly hissed at him.

"You're not intimidating a witness here and certainly not a young girl. Come, let's sit down here and you can tell us calmly what you know and what you spoke about," she continued with a gentle voice and pulled me to a chair by the table.

"Mr. Capuch, would you be so kind as to bring our witness a cup of tea also?" she asked Per in a tone of voice that established who had the say here.

Per turned red, but stood up and soon came back with a cup of tea.

"And now leave us alone," she spoke to Per in the same tone.

"Don't even think of it," he replied to my surprise in a quiet voice with a cold undertone.

"If you are interrogating my daughter, I will be present as her legal guardian."

Whoa there, what was that? I didn't recognize him like this at all.

"Then we'll take your daughter with us to the precinct and interrogate her there," snapped the sergeant. "And you'll come right along."

Per stood up and went around the table to the sergeant who had seated himself next to me and poked his index finger in his direction.

"You will neither take my daughter nor me to the precinct, but rather you will speak decently with all present here in my house. And if you should dare," he roared now, "question the child without me and furthermore in your office, I will be standing in front of your boss five minutes later with a pack of lawyers and a suit for damages, and you can depend on not having another peaceful moment. Then your pension will be just enough to pay for the postage on your resignation."

Boom. I was knocked flat and sat there with my mouth open. Had he just said "my daughter?" Per, who had treated me so snottily all these years, was prepared to take me into his protection? Wow, that was something!

The sergeant sat there and looked as if he would soon explode and gasped for breath.

"You can question my daughter," Per used the word again, "peacefully and decently here in my presence, but you will stick to the law and will not put the girl under pressure," he now turned to Mrs. Turgel in a quiet tone.

"You can bet on that," she answered and shot a withering look at Mr. Whiskey Keg.

From then on the conversation proceeded noticeably harmoniously and affably, because only Mrs. Turgel asked and the fat man with a beet-red face took notes.

I told her that I was ashamed that I hadn't met with Rose after the internship because I had had so much to do myself.

"She recently began to take riding lessons and you know how that is with young girls when they begin working with animals," Per interrupted me.

My amazement grew with every moment. Per wanted to help me over the terrible hurdle of explaining why I no longer had time for Rose. What was going on here?

The inspector got a dreamy expression on her face and sighed.

"Yes, yes, I know that...but now let us continue. Did Katharina, I mean did Rose ever speak to you about something that went beyond what you usually discussed?"

Something was rumbling in my stomach. There was something, but that was a secret and Rose had made me promise never to speak to anyone about it ever. But the promise was nipping and pinching my stomach.

Mrs. Turgel appeared to be able to read thoughts, "She made you promise not to speak to anyone about it," she asked in a quiet voice.

I winced.

"How do you know that? I stammered in a breathy voice.

"It is almost always like that when a girl wants to visit a family her parents does not know for the weekend and then doesn't come back on time. Most of the time a girlfriend is privy and they have given a mutual promise of eternal silence." Now she sounded sad.

"Well the promise is invalid, I can tell you, because we suspect that a crime has occurred," she stressed in a firm voice and looked directly at me with her cold eyes.

I began to tremble; I felt sick and had to hold onto the table. All of a sudden everything was spinning and I again felt this threat that I had sensed so often in the past few days.

With tears in my eyes, I continued to speak, "Before the internship she told me about a man whom she met in the Bengalese Gardens and who had offered her an internship."

"What is the guy's name and where does he live?" boomed from the direction of the fat sergeant.

"Shut your trap already and stop disrupting the interview, you boorish idiot, you..." Mrs. Turgel screeched in the direction of her colleague who now finally lost his composure.

His face turned gray, even the red bulb above his now open mouth no longer glowed and he collapsed like a balloon, in which one had stuck a pin. A Norwegian officer would never have spoken to a colleague in this tone, so I was now certain, that she had American roots.

Now with a gentle voice again, the policewoman continued to question me. At this point I felt I was in good hands with her and had the feeling that she would protect me from her people. For that reason I was startled when Per's face became more and more distrustful and he now said in an ice-cold voice, "Watch what you're doing. I see through your 'good guy – bad guy' games."

She threw him a withering look.

"Look, Jella," she continued, "Rose is gone and her mother is crying her eyes out. We have already asked everyone connected to her and no one has a clue. The only thing we can do is to follow up every clue, no matter how vague it is."

I nodded. We had beaten around the bush long enough.

"She spoke of this man when she was preparing for the internship. She appeared to be really in love. Rose is already seventeen; she is by far the oldest in our class, you know, and therefore she wanted to meet a boy. And now she just chose a man."

"A man? Does that mean that he was older?" Mrs. Turgel followed up.

"Yes, late thirties, she said. And that he reminded her of her father who has been gone a long time. And then she told me that he had already taken her out for dinner and brought her home from Drammen in a taxi. That must have been terribly expensive."

"Continue talking; tell us everything you can think of," prompted the officer when I faltered.

"Yes, and they wanted to meet again after the internship. Nathan, that's what she called him, told her that he owned an apartment in Oslo and if she wanted to visit him, he would pick her up and they could look at the city for a weekend and he would bring her back."

Breathless silence lay in the room. Now it slowly became clear to me what I was saying and what I had suppressed when Rose told me her story.

"Did Rose tell you where she met this Nathan?" she now asked.

"In the Bengalese Gardens, she said. He worked there as head of the rhododendron department."

"Huh? How do you spell that?" grunted the sergeant next to me. Apparently he had regained his strength.

"Write 'head of the department of the rose family,'" retorted Mrs. Turgel and raised her eyebrows. The guy was getting on her nerves.

"There is no Bengalese Garden in Drammen and also no botanical garden much less a rhododendron department. Was she perhaps speaking of the zoological park in Oslo?" she continued with a quiet voice.

Something lay in the air. Something was terribly wrong here. Why did the police not know that here was a Bengalese Garden in Drammen?

Now I stuttered, "but Rose did her internship there; everyone in school knew that. And it was certainly not the zoological park; they don't do any research there."

"Jella, we asked the teachers. It is true that she filled in the Bengalese Gardens in Drammen on her form. But this garden does not exist and never has."

From the other side, the fat sergeant now grumbled, "Jella, could it be that Rose deceived you? That she invented something to have time for a meeting with this 'Nathan' or whatever he is called?"

I was indignant. "Rose is my best friend and I am her only confidant in school. She only tells her mother more."

"She told her mother hat she was visiting a girlfriend named Ariana. Didn't she speak to you about that?"

Now the tears came. I shook my head. I felt so miserable I could no longer speak. Why had Rose entangled me in this web of lies?

"Can you describe the man; did Rose say anything about him?" I heard Mrs. Turgel quietly at my side.

I swallowed. She had said something, but it all sounded so strange that I didn't take it seriously.

"Jella, tell us everything, regardless whether it seems important or unimportant to you," said the policewoman in a sad, serious tone.

"Well, she said that he was tall and had blond hair like her father. And yes, I don't know if it will amount to anything, but she said he smelled exactly like her father when he used to come home from work in his blacksmith's shop. Sweaty and like metal."

I was a little ashamed to have voiced this small, intimate secret, but Mrs. Turgel just said, "Good, that will perhaps help us along. We'll finish for today; maybe we will interview you again, but then I will come alone," she continued, throwing an angry look in the direction of the sergeant. Both stood and took their leave.

After they were out, Per and I gazed after them. Before the two climbed into the police car, the fat one laid his arm around the inspector and gave her a hug. I was stunned.

Hadn't the two just hated each other with all their hearts?

Per grunted, "Just as I thought."

I didn't understand what he meant, but turned to him and said, "Thanks. That was really nice."

"Forget it," Per snapped back, now as unfriendly again as always.

"I'm certain that the luzo stuff let us in for this trouble." With that, he turned around and left the room.

Intimidated, confused, tired and sad, I crept up the wide stairs to my room. I turned on the light and then fell to my knees.

On my bed lay a rose. In the room it smelled like sweat, dirt and metal.

Departure from Hokksund

I awoke again. Outside it was pitch-dark. I lay on the floor in front of the bed, my head throbbed and I felt as sick as a dog. Slowly, I got up. The pillow was empty; no rose lay on it and the smell of man's sweat and iron had disappeared. The window was half-opened even though I knew I had closed it before I had gone away. I must have had a hallucination.

When I turned around, I saw Parilar outside my window in the moonlight. He looked up attentively and his tail twitched excitedly to and fro. That gave me new strength and I felt my self-confidence returning as I turned and went out.

Slowly I crept down the stairs; I had had enough of this house. Downstairs I flung my arms around Parilar and broke out in tears.

"There was a feeling of threatening danger, so I came here. And something is not right here," said my luzo as his tail twitched restlessly.

"You must mean the police car," I answered stammering through a veil of tears.

"Rose has disappeared and they are looking for her everywhere and so they questioned me."

"No, I saw that; they were not important to me. Something else here is fishy. Something stinks here in the truest sense of the word," he replied with a furrowed brow.

"It seems to me as if someone ran through here who hadn't washed in months."

I flinched.

"You're becoming pale all of a sudden," Parilar looked at me, concerned.

"When I came into my room this evening, a rose lay on my bed and smelled of sweat," I stuttered slowly.

The luzo reflected a moment. "Let's search the area; perhaps we'll find something that will help us."

I swung myself onto his back and we took off. Silently the cat circled over the park; we flew over the nearest treetops of the woods and searched the paths. Nothing was to be seen.

Except for a police car, but a different one than the one that had come to visit us today, which drove slowly on a forest road in the direction of Drammen. It was just strange that it was driving without lights.

Parilar turned off in the direction that the car was traveling and we tried to get a view of the inside without being seen ourselves. In the car sat two men; the driver wore a uniform. I thought I recognized Chief Inspector Louis Terzero. What was he doing here at this time of night? The car arrived at the main road, turned off toward the city, and then the lights turned on. It accelerated and we lost sight of it.

Wordlessly and thoughtfully, we flew back to the Capuchs' villa. I dismounted, went up to my room, packed up a few things and left the house. For the time being I didn't want to return. Parilar brought me to Tyrsenor and for the first time, I fell asleep on his back.

Lake Landuza

It was a cold morning and Fanres was already waiting for us with a luzo. I had never seen this luzo before. It had jet-black fur and cold yellow eyes that could teach you to fear if you looked for too long. His fur was already streaked with strands of gray. He was much larger and older than Parilar. The red skin of two major scars shimmered through his sleek fur.

Parilar gave the other luzo a friendly greeting but did not share, as was common among the cats, some nudges, instead lowering his head almost humbly. It appeared to be a special animal that enjoyed high esteem.

We had spent the previous night in a cave near the village and I had recovered well at the side of my companion. The energy that he emanated always let me regain my strength quickly. So, on this clear morning, the experiences of the last few days seemed to be a distant nightmare that no longer had meaning. I was looking forward to the adventures that now awaited me.

"Ready?" asked Fanres even before I could ask any questions. He was familiar with my curiosity and didn't want to lose time explaining any number of things to me.

I nodded in excitement and our luzos took off into the air.

It was a long flight to the lake. We first flew a short stretch north in the direction of the mountain slopes in order to then turn east over the archives building. At a dizzying height I could glance at the huge facility that was grouped in several high stories around a five-sided inner courtyard with a giant figure in the center. It was still dark on the ground and the rising sun blinded me so that I couldn't recognize the features.

From there, we followed a little river that was lined with gorgeous trees that dipped their long branches into the water. It gurgled over several low waterfalls into the valley, where it supplied the village with water. Soon the trees became denser and steep cliffs, over which the river cascaded in higher and higher falls, forced us further up. Behind a last high cliff, the ground evened out and we moved toward the brilliant reflective surface of Lake Landuza, which stretched to far beyond the horizon so that even at this height I couldn't make out the opposite shore. When we reached the huge body of water, the sun was already high in the sky and warmed us with its rays.

We landed in a small grove on the shore of the water. A group of old oaks stood in a circle around a grassy area. Not until we had almost landed did I discover a row of old columns supporting a low gabled roof in the shadows. From art class I knew the term for such columns and for that reason, my mouth dropped open full of amazement.

They were clearly Doric columns exhibiting a typical bulge in the middle. They even bore a triangular pediment on the gable end. They looked like Greek temples. According to that they must be ancient. How did they possibly get here?

In the center of the supports was a round enclosure built up out of almost white marble, from which the clearest water gurgled out of a flat drain into a channel to the lake. I looked into the fountain and saw that it enclosed a deep spring that bubbled to the top in a tempestuous movement. The spring brought hot water to the top. Before entering the lake, the wide rivulet flowed into a flat basin, where it combined with the sea water. Light clouds of steam arose where the water entered the lake.

I had heard many stories about the body of water from the village inhabitants during the past few weeks, but no one seemed to have set eyes on the lake. Anyone who spoke about it lowered his voice and whispered only vague information that gave the body of water a dark, mystical character. No one had told me about this grove.

At the lake, I knelt down and carefully stretched out my hand toward the water that appeared cold and deep, almost uncanny. But as I cautiously held out my hands, a comfortably warm wetness enveloped them. A strange scent, like violets, appeared to float over the water and at some distance, strange structures that one could easily have taken for faces at night, appeared through wafts of mist that drifted off the water's surface. But now in the sunlight, it was only mist. Or so I believed anyway.

"That is the holy grove of Lake Landuza," I heard Fanres' voice, who had remained standing at a respectful distance.

"Only a few people and luzos may approach it because the energy of the water is too powerful. One must take care, because gases get through the cracks in the ground that can throw people and luzos into ecstasy."

He pointed to a cone walled with stones that I first thought to be a column and out of which a weak veil rose upon closer observation.

"Doric columns, marble, leaking gas – this is like a new version of the Oracle of Delphi," I thought to myself as I went down to the lake. But the mood of the grove touched the deepest part of my soul and a feeling of awe spread through me.

The shore was overgrown with big old willows that lowered their branches deep into the water and for the most part covered the rocks and the winding gullies behind. Further up, a dense forest began, which primarily consisted of oaks and other smaller deciduous trees and which was replaced from a certain level on by a forest of black pines up to the edge of the unforested zone. In the morning light, the enormous crenalations of high mountains gleamed.

In the water that appeared turquoise up close, my hands were difficult to spot. The surface let hardly any light through although it looked clear. It was as if it swallowed up the light.

I started to love this water; it took me prisoner like a great passion. The smooth surface attracted me like a magnet. Most of all, I would have liked to immerse my head. Inside of me I heard a gentle hum, like an old forgotten children's song that unleashed unfamiliar longings in me. Slowly I drew closer and closer to the crystal liquid until I was suddenly pulled back.

"Stop! Don't dip in! That is dangerous. You can dip your hand in without reservation, but no more. Take in its power, but don't go any closer," said Fanres with a firm voice.

Too bad; the water had awakened deep feelings in me; it attracted me magically. But my escort was clear and precise and so I held myself to his directions.

Fanres sat down on a tree stump on the shore and closed his eyes appreciatively.

I tried to do the same. But the clear element still attracted me. It was not easy for me to resist this pull. Just once to simply immerse my head!

Dreamily I played with the pendant that was still dangling around my neck, while Fanres still held his eyes half shut trance-like and savored the peace of the lake.

All at once I became very thirsty. I was already permitted to dip in my hand; then I would probably also be permitted to scoop up some of the water. And so I filled my hollow hand with clear lake water and trickled it slowly into my mouth. It tasted wonderful! I took another handful and then another.

Until I heard Fanres say, "Not too much at once; it can sometimes cause extraordinary effects."

I now likewise closed my eyelids and surrendered to the pictures that now appeared to my inner eye.

Suddenly a gentle wind arose that rippled the surface of the water and triggered a powerful rushing; it sounded like a seething. When I perceived that, I opened my eyes again. Strangely enough, only a small part of the lake was in motion, like a line. A wave pulled itself from the place in the pool where I had scooped up water, across the lake in the direction of the mist.

There, where it met the wall of fog, the billows parted. Shapes emerged from the blurred veil. At first they looked like a large mountain; then I recognized an island. But this island floated over the water!

It seemed to me like a Fata Morgana, strangely unreal, infinitely far away and at the same time quite near. Far away I saw white specks that were probably villages or cities, a dense forest stretched from the shore almost to the peak.

I was greatly scared when I quite suddenly saw tongues of fire shoot out of the peak of the island and then glowing lava rolled down the slopes. My heart raced; a chill ran up my back.

As if through a telescope I became aware that ships were breaking away from the island. They hoisted black sails and traveled away in a straight line. From the distance they looked like little toy boats. The masts moved as if in a storm and the line that the ships had maintained at first dispersed; the fleet scattered. Most of the ships soon disappeared behind the horizon.

Yet one continued to travel in our direction and rapidly became larger. As if driven by a hurricane, it raced toward us, the black sails swept out; the bow dipped deep into the foaming lake; sea foam sprayed high over the deck.

I froze to a pillar of salt. The boat would crash on the shore of the lake and shatter. And carry Fanres and me with it!

I wanted to scream and run away, but no sound escaped my lips; I stood there as if frozen fast. My heart raced in my chest; my lips trembled; my knees became weak.

In the next moment the ship was in front of us – and raced right through me! I only felt a weak impact. Like from a strong gust of wind; then it was over.

But I was still in shock.

When the ship had arrived at my level, I had seen something horrible.

A hand came over the ship's side; then another, and then I suddenly saw many people jumping over the side of the ship. All were dressed in black robes, their heads hidden under deep hoods.

In the short time, I had seen that so distinctly that I now involuntarily turned around and looked for the people.

Nothing was to be seen, No ship, no hooded people, no creatures. Fanres sat on a rock on the shore, eyes closed, and everything around us was dead silent. Right and left behind Fanres sat both luzos, who had returned noiselessly from the woods, like two statues on hind legs. They also held their eyes closed and didn't move.

And it just now occurred to me that nothing was moving. Not a leaf rustled on the trees, not a tree trunk swayed in the wind. Everything seemed to be frozen fast, no sound, no movement, no twittering of birds, nothing.

I turned my head again to the lake and saw full of dismay that the island, on which the volcano had erupted, was slowly sinking into the lake, breaking apart into two pieces. Huge waves spread out to all sides.

But the perspectives were such that I just now became aware that the island was not in Lake Landuza, but instead in a vast ocean. This lake just brought the picture of the demise to the surface. The lava flowed in enormous red streams into the ocean and immense plumes of steam arose. They now mixed with the fog over lake Landuza and pushed in front of the gruesome scene like a curtain.

What I had seen was an event from another time; that was now clear to me. And with it I felt a message had arrived to me but whose content I did not understand. What was it supposed to mean; why did I witness this secret?

Suddenly I felt Parilar's warm breath at my side. He looked at me; in his eyes I again saw the eerie green gleam that I had already seen once when I found out where we were. I felt that I once again had contact with the strange being that made use of Parilar.

Still trembling from the gruesome picture of the sinking island, I gathered my courage. "What's the meaning of this?" I sent my question through the bond with Parilar.

And again I perceived the deep, dark voice, "This is supposed to show you the way."

"But what kind of way is that supposed to be?" I probed. Now I wanted answers to my questions and to no longer be palmed off. And so I struggled to sort my thoughts and formulate questions that would finally enlighten me.

"What you saw happened a long time ago. It is the cause of everything that has happened and will occur. Parilar is the only one in this generation who has the power to convey my messages and for that reason he is at your side."

"Who are you?" I asked and even over the bond, my question sounded fearful and squeaky.

For endless seconds nothing happened. Then I heard the voice again, but it became quieter and appeared to go away, "The lake is our connection, an old volcano...the power...I...am...trapped...the way...look for...release..."

And then it was gone. I no longer heard it and met no response to my questions. And it sounded as if I were calling into a deep cave.

I was sad. Instead of receiving answers, I had seen shocking scenes as real as if they had taken place directly before my eyes. And I still didn't know who was speaking to me through Parilar. And what the whole thing was supposed to mean. And...

Parilar awakened me from my trance. He pressed his strong body gently to my side as if he wanted to console me.

Slowly I turned around and noticed that Fanres and his luzo still sat frozen in place. Time seemed to stand still for them. Parilar looked at me and said over the band, now with his own voice, "I know that I can and should establish contact. But I still don't know more than you. I have also already posed questions, but I am still stuck for an answer. But I do know this much: We should begin the search."

"But what should we look for and why?" I retorted exasperated.

"I don't know that either. I only sense that the lake is the connection. It was formerly a volcano. And it was connected to other volcanoes. That's where its enormous energy comes from. I often come here to refuel; it is the source of the energy that I need to break through time and space."

Behind me I perceived a rustling. Fanres and his luzo were moving again and I now heard the twittering of birds and the sounds of the woods again. Fanres stood up, came to me, looked at me and asked curtly, "Did you have visions?"

I nodded and then it bubbled out of me, what I had seen. I told him about the island, about the ships, about my great fear. But I didn't mention the voice that spoke to me through Parilar. Somehow I sensed that this was something I should keep to myself.

Fanres slowly shook his head to and fro and gave me the following explanation:

"Zaron sent us here because he wanted to know whether there were any other powers in you that could be of use to us. Most of the village inhabitants don't come here because the energy of the lake numbs them. Only luzos and the riders of the Great Five as well as some chosen ones from the council manage to endure the power of the lake.

In every generation of the Great Five there is now one exceptional person who is in the position of receiving messages. In the last generation this was Beleia who unfortunately left us. In our new group we couldn't find anyone who receives visions here. Therefore Zaron wanted to make a last attempt with you, although it didn't sit well with him. That is, the council talked him into it. Now we know that you are the one who can convey messages from the holy grove."

I was now astonished; how was that possible? Until a few weeks ago, I was just a normal student and now I occupied a special role already?

"What is the meaning of these visions? And what did Beleia report?"

"The pictures are similar. She also spoke of the demise of a whole world; the pictures must have rattled her very much. She also said that we would be protected by the lake; only very powerful magic could polarize its energy enough to make its protective shield to disappear. That agrees with what is reported in the codices Zaron says, who is the only one who can read them.

Take some of the liquid; it will provide you the additional energy, but take care that it is not too much."

When we set out again in the afternoon, I knew where the odd energy that shielded Tyrsenor from the surrounding world originated. It was the water of the lake that emitted magical powers and which gave energy and protection to all who allowed themselves to be charmed by it.

Longingly I looked back over Lake Landuza. Sometime I would visit it again and get to the bottom of its secret; I swore that to myself!

Our luzos had likewise enjoyed the morning. They had rested at the edge of the lake a while longer and held their eyes closed. One paw lay in the water, but heads remained raised high. So they lay there like statues. When I climbed on Parilar's back, I sensed how his newly gained energy engulfed me.

The theft

Shortly before we reached Tyrsenor we heard screaming and yelling from afar and I saw luzos rushing to rise into the sky. People ran back and forth as if bitten by a snake and called something to one another.

I had never seen such confusion. Frightened, I looked at Fanres who was looking down concerned. Something terrible must have happened in our absence.

"The codices!" Fanres' luzo immediately raced off in the direction of the main square and Parilar stayed at the tip of his tail. He had never before flown so fast!

The whole village was now assembled on the square. Zaron stood on the stone pedestal like on the day of my first arrival when he had led the ceremony for my entrance into the community.

"Quiet! I ask you all to be silent! Corey, come and report what has happened," Zaron commanded in a loud voice.

Corey clambered onto the pedestal and his gaze wandered over the assembled company.

"I was keeping the intermediate watch in front of the secret room what I suddenly heard something. A rustling, then it was still. Naturally, I promptly checked it out but no one was to be found in the room. But one of the safes of our shrine stood wide open, empty! The first part of the codices is now completely lost."

So up to now only a small piece of the first part of the codices had been missing. Apparently the thief had returned to steal further parts! Loud murmuring and frightened cries rang out.

I myself quivered with rage and tears rose in my eyes: I belonged to those who were supposed to protect the codices. Now I stood here feeling helpless and angry!

"Tonight the room will be under extra guard and the patrols will be reinforced. All present return immediately to your houses and stay there until I personally give the all-clear!" Zaron commanded.

Lesla hurried through the crowd to me and we went together into her house. Parilar and Jali followed us.

96

"Do you think it was someone from our village?" Lesla asked when we sat on her bed.

"I haven't the foggiest notion," I answered. Lost in thought I called forth my dreams again. In one of the first dreams my mother had opened a secret door and had disappeared with the stolen documents unnoticed!

All at once I knew how the thief could escape unnoticed! He was familiar with the secret door.

"Lesla, I know where the codices are now, come along!" Not comprehending, she stared at me.

I tried to quickly describe to her everything that I had seen in my dreams. She just looked at me with wide eyes, but didn't say anything. At least she followed me wordlessly and we left our luzos in the room, who for their part fiercely protested. But they would simply be too noticeable; now they would only be a hindrance.

Unseen, we managed the way through dark alleys to the main building, that stood there completely unlit from the outside. Twice we had to hide ourselves from patrolling guards, at which Lesla turned out to be an ingenious beguiler. Crouched low, we crept through a side entrance and then through a half-darkened hallway that was only illuminated by a few flickering candles. It continued over wide stairs, winding passageways and large wooden doors that creaked loudly when we opened them. But we continued to be unnoticed. A few minutes later my memories from the dreams had led me to the secret room.

When we peered around the last corner, I saw that Lacato kept guard and groaned inwardly. We were out of our league. I just wanted to whisper to Lesla that our plan would lead nowhere when she stumbled and fell directly into Lacato's arms, who stared at her with a strange look.

"What are you doing here? Zaron will flip out if he finds out. Go back home," he warned.

But apparently it had not been unpleasant for him to hold Lesla in his arms. I couldn't refrain from a suppressed giggle.

"He won't find out unless you squeal on us. Jella, come out; we can trust him."

Oh great, what else? Groaning I retreated from my hiding place and Lesla began to immediately tell Lacato everything that she had learned from me. An uneasy feeling crept over me.

"You really have these dreams?" Lacato asked me quizzically, still holding Lesla in his arms.

I nodded and pointed as proof to the necklace I wore around my neck.

"Hmmm...okay, I trust you. But don't cause any damage and not a word to anyone!"

Lesla let out a squeal and thankfully gave him a kiss on the cheek. I believe I saw Lacato's face turn red, smiled in embarrassment and followed her.

"Be careful!" we heard Lacato's warning voice behind us.

The secret chamber was only the entrance into a further building in the giant complex. We first climbed a grand stairway that led directly into a room with high ceilings.

At the back end of the room was a large set of double doors that led into a smaller room. There we found a small door leading to a larger hall.

We stood in exactly the same room that I had seen in my dreams. On the front side hung the picture of the luzo that I had seen in my dreams and which appeared even bigger here than I remembered it. With decisive steps I approached the portrait.

Lesla clung to my arm in excitement and looked expectantly over my shoulder when I tried to push the painting to the side. It didn't budge from the spot. Why had it just looked so easy in the dream?

Now it occurred to me that the painting didn't look as if it were painted on canvas. It was made of metal and apparently so tightly attached to the back wall of the room that there were no gaps to be found. It appeared to be impossible to move this picture even only an inch, because it was more stable than any door to a safe.

I thought for a moment. What had happened in the dream so that my mother could shift this portrait so easily? She had run her right hand along under the frame. Then she had moved slightly to the side and touched another place on the picture with her left hand, pressing her upper body against a certain spot.

I did the same as she had. On the lower frame I found a depression that was equipped with a strange embossment. I was irritated when I felt it.

Somehow the engraving seemed to be familiar, but I couldn't place it, so I asked Lesla quietly.

She touched the spot and said after a while, "Those are the holy symbols from the pillar; I think you have to touch them in the right order."

And I did that. When I was finished a soft sound came from the picture. At first we were frightened and jumped back a bit. But then we pulled ourselves together and I went to the left side of the picture. My dream-I had pressed her upper body against a certain spot.

When I looked there, I saw that there was a small image of the pillar under the raised left paw of the luzo, which we could only recognize up close. I pulled the chain around my neck to the side to get closer to the picture and pressed my body against this spot.

Nothing happened. The sound stopped and the picture could not be moved. I was deeply disappointed. But we tried again; every time at a different spot, every time without success. The last time I forgot in my growing exhaustion to move the chain aside and therefore touched the pillar with the silver pendant.

A dull bang resounded throughout the room, the picture quivered and we both shook along with it, we were so terrified.

But now it was quite easy to pull it to the side. It had been the contact with the silver pendant that had opened the way for us!

A cold draft seeped out of a dark opening behind the painting, making me shudder.

"Go ahead, what are you waiting for?" urged Lesla. I made an effort and pushed myself into the darkness. Lesla followed me.

We came into a murky tunnel. Already after a short distance the light from the entrance dimmed and it became pitch-dark. Carefully we lowered ourselves to all fours and began to crawl, feeling our way along the wall of the narrow passageway. At first, we went straight ahead for a few minutes; then I whacked my head on a wall. Frightened, I felt around, relieved to find out that the passageway broke off to the right. So we scrambled further, from time to time taking some spider webs along, which I wiped off of my face, snorting.

Doing so, I then suddenly lost my grip and tumbled into a pit. Thank God, it wasn't too deep, 7 feet at most, but nevertheless I had hit my head hard.

"Where are you?" I heard Lesla's frightened voice above me.

"Down here, watch out so that you don't fall, there is a pit here," I replied ill-tempered.

I touched the walls and felt around for an opening. In front of me, I was indeed able to find a wide passageway. When I searched the wall further, I felt notches in the walls that led upwards in a row. There were footholds in the masonry. "I could have made my way without bumps and bruises," I thought annoyed.

At first I wanted to climb up again until a thought came, "Can you feel if there's a way to go further up there?" I called up. I heard Lesla's searching shuffle and then her voice.

"This is the end up here. I can only find the hole next to me."

"You can climb down; there are footholds in the wall; try to feel them with your feet," I called up.

A short while later, first one object then another smacked my mistreated head. Lesla's shoes, as I discovered after my initial shock.

"What are you doing there; why are you throwing your boots at me?" I whined angrily.

"I can find the foothold better without shoes; otherwise I'm afraid I'll miss them and fall on your head," came back from the floor above me.

"That's all I would need, for the two of us to kill one another," I thought and scrambled precautiously further into the passageway next to me.

Shortly thereafter, I was with Lesla again and she was united with her boots. That accomplished, we continued our search, this time a bit more carefully.

We had already been crawling about fifteen minutes and I wanted to suggest that we turn around when the cold draft became stronger and a sound like rushing water hinted at the end of the eerie path. We immediately quickened our scrambling, eager to leave the stuffy narrowness. In front of us, a thick grate blocked the way, but it was easy to open. Someone had broken the lock.

Greedily I inhaled the fresh night air when we finally arrived outside, covered in dirt. Now we could see something again. In a diffused twilight we recognized that after a sharp turn, the narrow tunnel ended at a steep slope which we slid down on the seat of our pants.

From the bottom we could just make out that the low entrance opened into a large cave. Even if clueless souls had strayed here, they would hardly be able to find this opening. And this being would have to be a good climber also, because it seemed almost impossible to get back up the slippery slope.

A scare flashed through me: How were we supposed to get back again? But I suppressed the thought; what counted now was finding the codices again.

Carefully I looked around. We had landed in a limestone cave. Oddly enough one could make out the walls and the ceiling. I was taken aback when I saw the source of light. A small waterfall rushed down the side wall through narrow channels and disappeared into a crack in the floor. The water shone with a soft yellow glow, and the drops that splashed when it hit obstacles glistened in all colors and sent a warm light into the huge cave. A strange scent of violets and myrrh awakened memories in me and all at once it became clear that the water must come from Lake Landuza.

The light was enough to illuminate the area and we saw that the room was as big as the inside of a cathedral. All around us white and light brown colored stalagmites grew high and tried to unite with stalactites that reached down from the ceiling.

"I believe the thief fled in this direction!" Lesla pointed to the back wall of the cave whose outlines could now be made out. At the far end we vaguely recognized a passage. We crept closer and saw a further passageway that disappeared in darkness. And then another and another and...

At first my mouth remained open. In front of us lay a tangle of passageways and shafts that all led into darkness.

"Well, lots of fun searching!" I thought to myself. It promised to become a long night. Above all, because it seemed nearly impossible to find a trail on the hard limestone in the murky tunnels.

"This is the way," cried Lesla excited and pointed to a low tunnel.

"And why are you so certain about it?" I asked doubtingly.

She calmly shrugged her shoulders and said it was her instinct. But what else should we do? So, on through the middle! That is, into the opening. And already after a few moments I had gained respect for Lesla's instinct.

She had led us into a dark opening and after we had escaped the attempts of the thin stalactites on the ceiling to spear us, I saw in the waning twilight a path in front of us that led us safely through all further turnoffs and over shafts and cracks.

Even I could now see the small broken off stalactite tips that the thief had left behind on his escape. This someone had probably not counted on being followed and consequently didn't take care to cover his trail.

Without a sound, we followed the trail and after a few minutes came to the entrance of a low hall not bigger than a church. To the sides, further galleries and tunnels went off leading away upwards as well as downwards.

"There!" Lesla whispered to me and pointed to the middle of the cave.

Someone cowered there behind a wide limestone basin. It was a man whose posture seemed strangely familiar to me. He rustled with something that lay on the floor and giggled without ceasing. His light hair stood out from his head in wild bushes. All at once he breathed in with a hiss; he had sensed something. Abruptly he turned his head in our direction and Lesla dug her fingernails into my arm.

The filthy dirty man had discovered us. He came closer and I recognized his face. Terrified and amazed at the same time I opened my eyes wide. It was the man who had murdered my father in my dream: Gribor! Fear crept up my spine. This man was dangerous!

"Who do we have here? Two courageous pursuers who want to catch the thief?"

It sounded more like a conclusion than a question. His deep scratchy voice echoed from the cave walls which made the situation seem even uncannier. Now he stood directly in front of us and his stinking breath stuck in my nose.

Yet I remained standing motionlessly.

"A pity that you'll not be able to tell anyone about your discovery."

Slowly Gribor pulled a knife out of his pants pocket and grinned demonically.

Lesla uttered a cry of terror and shrank back. I, however, remained standing. I wanted Lesla to run back and get help.

"Run and get help, fast," I whispered to her and took a step forward. Completely to Gribor's surprise, I placed a well-aimed punch on his chest that made him stumble backwards, and my opponent lost his balance for a short time.

102

Enough time for Lesla who I heard disappear behind me into the passageways. Before Gribor could catch himself again, I hustled a bit to the right into a murky gallery. As far away from him as possible.

But Gribor had picked himself up again quickly, ran after me and had soon caught up to me.

I was frantic and didn't know what I could do. So I turned around and raised my hands fearfully. Gribor took a lunge toward me. I immediately saw the knife flashing. Reflexively I pivoted into my opponent, used the side of my hand to hit the arm holding the handle of the knife and then avoided him. The knife disappeared in a high arc behind a block of rock.

The practices on the village square were paying off. I rejoiced inwardly and believed to have withstood the worst of it. But I had grossly underestimated this man. Now everything went furiously fast.

He jumped at me, feet first, shoved me to the ground and dealt me a kick in the gut that caused a hellish pain and took my breath away. Then he bolted behind the rock, found the knife faster than I would have liked and came at me with it.

I couldn't move; his kick had dazed me so much. I couldn't get my breath; I held my hands over my hurting belly and tried to get air again. Gasping, I pressed my hand into my body and tried to get up. But my legs didn't want to obey me. My eyes were wide open and in panic-stricken fear I saw Gribor slowly getting closer, again donning his demonic grin.

"Oh, yes, before I forget it: You were an outstanding guide, Jella!"

My panic gave way to confusion for a moment. What did he mean with 'guide'? And how did he know who I was?

"Thanks to you I could locate everyone because many years have passed since I was last with the luzos. I would have gotten lost if Louis hadn't helped me."

Louis? What did Louis have to do with the whole thing? Gribor seemed to be sure of his prey because a malicious laugh came out of his mouth as he slowly came closer. And with relish, he took the time to explain when he saw my confused face, "Louis is a good old friend of mine, because after my flight back then I lived in the other world with a luzo that I met in the mountains after it had found a way. My old luzo did not want to come along because it was sworn to Zaron's predecessor and also had no chance of breaking through the wall of energy. I asked Louis to watch you. Luckily everything went spontaneously when you told him about your internship. At the end, he wanted to drive you home, isn't it true? So that he knew where you lived and could easily shadow you."

I took a sharp breath. And diagnosed, "So the ankle cuff came from him, too?"

Gribor laughed narcissistically, "One can look at it that way, too. I borrowed it myself and fastened it around your foot when you were slumbering deeply and soundly. You house urgently needs to be made burglar-proof. When you and your luzo flew back, I could follow you up to the wall of fog. Behind it, the ankle cuff was no longer effective, because these devices don't function in this world. But the two of you fooled around and caused such noise that I only had to follow the din."

I trembled; all this was too much. Then Gribor took a swipe at me and let the knife hurtle down at me. A brutal pain went through my shoulder. I held my hand on the site of the bleeding and distorted my face screaming.

My shoulder hurt severely, but he had only wounded me slightly. His blow had traveled from above to below and was apparently only intended to frighten me. I was at first bewildered. Did he want to torture me slowly?

A picture appeared to my inner eye of how Gribor stabbed my father and all of a sudden a cold rage got into me and I had the strength to sit up. I jumped up and raised my hands to deflect the next blow.

At the same moment I noticed a movement and determined with horror that Lesla had not taken off, but was creeping up on Gribor from behind. She wanted to protect me!

Too late I realized that Gribor was following my gaze and reacted fast as lightening. He turned around and stabbed out. Lesla's body slumped lifelessly in front of him. He had stabbed her!

I screamed loudly in my distress; horrified I realized what had happened here and jumped to Lesla, where I knelt down and took her in my arms. But there was no sign of life to be felt. How could that happen? Why Lesla, why did she of all people have to die? Why had Gribor only wounded me and not killed me too?

All of this was my fault. If I hadn't begun to describe my dreams to her and encouraged her to find the thief with me, all of this wouldn't have happened! And what happened with Jali now? Tears streamed down my face.

From the corner of my eye, I saw Gribor coming closer. When I turned around, he held the bloody knife in front of my face. I was certain that he would now kill me, too. A cold peace gripped me; if it was to be that I had to die here, then at least in battle!

But Gribor didn't strike out. "Listen, and listen closely." His words came to my ear as if through a dark filter. My sight disappeared though a veil of tears.

Again I perceived his voice and this time a cold shudder ran up my back.

"If you want to see Rose again, you will get me the other part of the codices and the exact pages that I need."

I believed I must have heard wrong. With my sleeve, I wiped the tears from my face.

"Say that again," I heard myself say.

"You understood me correctly." His voice appeared to drip poison; he had an ice-cold grin on his lips.

"I snatched Rose to get close to you. Because when Louis had found out that you had something to do with Catleya, I had to try to find you. And so I borrowed your girlfriend to have something in hand. It was pretty easy to convince her to come along. I believe she was in love with me."

His laugh resounded and he cockily smacked his thigh with his free hand.

My heart constricted. I felt my rage rise. No, it was more like ice cold hate. This person was not only the worst enemy of my parents; he had also kidnapped my best companion and before my eyes had murdered Lesla, of whom I had grown fond in the past few weeks! Incapable of making a decision, I had to continue to listen to his words.

"So, here's the deal: You will get me the part of the codices that describes the means by which one can acquire power. As soon as I have them, you will see Rose again." With these words he suddenly disappeared into a passageway.

In my state of shock I began to run around looking for help. Where were we here? How could I get out again? I tried to establish a connection to Parilar. In vain! In my panic and distress, I could not find the necessary peace to concentrate on the voice I could use to call him. And how could he get here? We were deep under the mountains and a luzo would only be able to navigate the passages with difficulty.

My gaze immediately fell upon flat sheets lying around that looked like unrolled documents, but made completely of a gleaming silver metal. When I picked them up, I comprehended what they were. They were as light as paper, flexible and smooth and covered with the same characters that I already knew from the column. At least one page of the texts, the other was in a readable script, but in a language I did not know.

A part of the codices! Trembling with pain, I held them in my hand and floundered. My shoulder throbbed and I felt myself becoming weaker and weaker. My sight kept swimming until everything around me finally went black.

Escape

Warm breath grazed my face and I heard someone quietly snorting: Parilar!

Smiling, I opened my eyes and would have preferred to close them again and forget what had happened. I lay on a cot; my shoulder was bandaged, and the moon shone in through a tiny barred window.

Wait a minute, barred window? Irritated, I sat up and immediately regretted it. My head felt like a herd of buffalos had trampled on it. Slowly, I took in my surroundings and was sorry that I had opened my eyes. Parilar and I were stuck in a tiny chamber with only a sink, a pit latrine and the sleeping accommodation on which I lay. Parilar sat on the stone floor and looked at me with concern.

"What happened?" I croaked in a weak voice.

"After you left, we waited. Surely three hours or even longer, but you didn't come back. All of a sudden, Jali winced and screamed out in pain. I didn't know what I should do; Jali was really not doing well and I decided – also for your safety – to tell Zaron what you had planned. He determined immediately that something must have happened to Lesla. As a result, he took off with a few fighters to look for you."

Parilar took a deep breath; then he continued, "At dawn, Zaron returned, and to everyone's dismay, he carried the dead Lesla with him and ...you. Luckily you were only unconscious. In any case, Zaron locked us in here, and said I should inform you to think over what you could add in your defense. What they did with Lesla and Jali, I don't know. Everything went so fast!"

We were silent for a while. Then I asked, "Do you know what Zaron meant with his words?"

Parilar shrugged his shoulders and replied, "I have no idea; at any rate, he did not look at you with kindness or concern. More like...a criminal."

I shuddered at these words. A criminal? Me?

But what crime was I supposed to have committed?

Cold moonlight shone cheerlessly into our cell. The pain and now also an empty stomach prevented me from thinking. It appeared to have been an eternity since I had eaten a decent meal. But I would probably have to wait a long time for that.

At some point, after further hours of waiting, a guard brought bread and water into our cell. It was impossible to get anything out of this stubborn fellow because he completely ignored us and our questions. He didn't even dignify us with a look. He was also not intimidated by Parilar who certainly could have knocked him down with a little jostle and set us free. The luzo, however, had too much respect for Zaron to even been able to conceive of the idea.

"Where did Zaron put the second half of the recovered Codices?"

Parilar looked at me uncomprehending. "The second half? I have no idea; it's probably still in the hands of the cunning thief."

I looked at Parilar in amazement. "But the book was lying next to me. Gribor didn't take it with him again."

Baffled, Parilar looked at me with wide eyes. "But why else did Zaron lock us in here if you had the book?"

"You think he believes that I stole the Codices, and that's why he locked us in here?"

"Could be, why else..." I didn't allow Parilar to finish.

"Then he also believes that I murdered Lesla and planned to take off with the Codices!" I realized, appalled.

Parilar looked at me in alarm. "I didn't see it that way. Probably he believes as well that I kept guard over Jali long enough, or worse yet detained him, until you had the Codices. As it is, he was annoyed that I chose someone outside of Tyrsenor as my rider. Now he probably considers his mistrust confirmed."

Groaning, I let myself slide to the floor. How could everything have come to this? Why, for heaven's sake, did everything have to be so complicated? Toward evening, Parilar and I still had no plan. We desperately had to speak to Zaron. And would he even listen to us?

In the middle of the night, I woke up in a bath of sweat. I had heard something. A rattling, then a creak. The cell door stood wide open. Straining, I stared into the darkness and could make out the outlines of a shape.

"Hello, who's there?" I whispered in a hoarse voice.

"Psst, it's me, Lacato. Come along, but be careful not to make any noise."

Stunned, I stood on my wobbly legs.

"Lacato? What are you doing here?"

"Be quiet. I've come to get you out of here, but if you keep on making noise, then they'll catch both of us."

Without asking further questions, Parilar and I tiptoed after him. The luzo, too, had enough of the imprisonment and in the meantime, his respect for Zaron was less than his desire for freedom.

We stumbled through the pitch-black hallways and stairways, where I would have gotten lost on my own, but Lacato led us safely through a small door into the fresh air.

"Where are we?" I looked around. But I couldn't even remotely orient myself.

"I have led you to a back exit. You were in the basement of the main building three floors under the holy room. A patrol only comes past the back side here every two hours. And now see that you get out of here. I have packed some food, but I can't do any more for you."

Thankfully, I hugged him. My eyes filled with tears of exhaustion and fatigue. I saw that he had tear-stained eyes as well. Lesla's death seemed to have hit him hard.

"Thank you. I will never forget this." I swung myself onto Parilar's back and accepted the bag of food.

"See you soon!" I said to him.

"I hope not. The whole village is against you at the moment; I believe you'd best not show your face here again so soon. And what I'm doing here, I'm doing for Lesla. She trusted you unconditionally."

I bit my lower lip. The whole village! It *was* possible for it to get worse.

"Do you believe I killed Lesla?"

"No, otherwise I definitely wouldn't have helped you. But I am probably the only one who is sticking by you. Everyone really liked Lesla, and it is difficult to say goodbye to her. No one believed that the time of the Great Five would end so soon! And now for the second consecutive time in successive generations."

His gaze darkened, and I felt that he was afraid of what lay in store for the village. I shuddered at his words. The time of our generation of the Great Five was indeed ended. Someone had succeeded in destroying the mythical protection of Tyrsenor that had saved it from the hostile world surrounding it. And now they were helplessly at the mercy of the danger. And all because of my dreams. Why, of all things, did I have to chase after Gribor? I decided to tell Lacato how everything had happened. He had earned it!

"It was Gribor. He could find us by following us, that is, Parilar and me. He stole the rest of the first part of the Codices and murdered Lesla. Where he fled, I don't know. But before I became unconscious, I still had the Codices with me. Someone must have taken them because Zaron doesn't have them."

Lacato let everything sink in. Then he nodded thoughtfully. "Yes, that sounds logical. Something like that fits him. Maybe Gribor took the rest of the Codices with him again when you were unconscious. But in your place, I would wait to tell Zaron everything. Everyone is pretty upset at the moment. Go now, soon a luzo patrol will come by here again and your scent must be gone by then. Hurry!"

I nodded in agreement and gave Parilar a sign. High in the sky, I turned around once more, but Lacato had disappeared.

Stars

A biting wind whipped my hair into my face and I clung on tighter to Parilar's warm and comforting body. The sun had almost gone down and had spilled its last light on the earth.

We had already been in the air since dawn. Parilar had turned north since our takeoff. He was certain that we would find a clue there to help us along.

We had flown off over the high mountains without generating a wall of fog. Thus we remained in this world. After the high peaks, the hillsides sank down into endlessly vast forests without any sign of human settlement.

My legs had fallen asleep; my fingers were numb, but Parilar flew and flew.

"Can't you stop flying already? Please!" My fatigue was now stronger that the fear that had driven us away from the village.

"As you wish..."

Relieved, I sighed and relaxed my cramped legs. Without any prior warning, Parilar's wings stopped beating and we rushed swiftly toward the hard earth.

"Parilar, what is wrong? Are you injured? Why are you no longer flying?" I shrieked. In my fear, I dug my fingernails into Parilar's neck and he roared in pain.

Then he began to hectically beat his wings once again. We floated above the trees again and now also over green meadows. Whew, that had been close! Was I relieved. I had already seen us smashed on the ground.

"What was wrong?" I asked, still gasping for air.

Parilar breathed as irregularly as I did. "There was nothing wrong with me. I just did what you asked: I stopped flying. Man, that was a trip! I would like to repeat that!"

"Don't you dare! I meant you should land and not simply stop beating your wings! Don't do something like that again. That was hell!"

"I would have slowed down in time, no worries. But if you wouldn't like to repeat it, I will of course refrain."

Thankfully I patted Parilar's neck and we sank to the earth. Even now, in this difficult situation, this cat was up for mischief. Sometimes his fun side surfaced at the completely wrong time...

111

We landed gently on the floor of the forest and Parilar pulled in his wings. Curiously he looked around and gave the all-clear signal. There was no danger here at the moment.

I myself didn't have the slightest idea where we were located and left the lead to Parilar.

"I smell water!" He had pursed his lips and sniffed in the air.

"We will rest by the water." Without a sound, Parilar crept to a small creek that was babbling along merrily.

It did me good to be able to move my legs. I looked up at the ancient dark fir trees. We would have to hurry if we wanted to eat by daylight. I gathered the foodstuffs together and shook out the contents. Lacato had given us a bottle of water, two loaves of bread, a piece of cheese, dried fruit and dried wild boar ham. We decided to deal with our provisions sparingly. Who knew how long we would have to wander around? I didn't want to be alone just now, and therefore Parilar didn't go out hunting either.

Tomorrow we would fly further until we had at some point found shelter where it would be possible us to live for an extended period of time. How it would proceed then, I myself didn't know yet.

The next morning I awoke with a thumping headache and my injured shoulder felt numb and swollen. My legs were wind burned from the long ride and my stomach was empty. I missed Lesla tremendously and my heart was heavy with grief.

I washed myself at the brook and sat on a fallen tree for a quick breakfast and to give thought to what to do next. In the process I dozed off again.

"Do you hear that?" Parilar suddenly jumped up happily excited.

"No, what?" I rubbed the sleep from my eyes and shook myself.

"I believe I hear a storm approaching from a distance..."

I strained to listen. Indeed, far back at the horizon gusts of wind were roaring over the treetops. I sat up and felt the high humidity. If we were in luck, a real tornado would develop from the harmless airstreams.

"Come, let's fly after the storm!"

This time we were not in luck. It was a funnel cloud. That means that the typical air turbulence doesn't reach the ground, as is the case with a tornado. And, in addition, we could not see the funnel cloud very well because there was no dust, rubble or debris on the perfect patch of grass over which the storm now moved. Without absorbing dirt, the eddy was scarcely recognizable.

Disappointed, we now flew several more hours to the north, always following the storm. We glided on through the air until we found ourselves over a large patch of grass at midday and made a stop. New storm clouds were already rumbling above us.

And this time we were indeed in luck. The thunderstorm sent huge towers of clouds into the clear sky at breathtaking speeds, and we didn't have to wait all that long for a mother cloud to lower its trunk to the earth and suck up complete loose clumps of earth making it visible. In the meantime, more and smaller tornados became visible raging around the mother cloud.

I observed the spectacle for a moment; then we finally took off. Parilar and I chased through the storm clouds, and the tornado whirled with us. Again and again, Parilar freed himself only to then fly with the mother cloud again for fun.

Several small tornados were always scattered around and then came the climax. One last time the storm flared and showed its full power, finally collapsing in a last rebellion.

"That was a tornado! It lasted long, more than ten minutes: I marveled and brushed my tousled hair out of my face.

Parilar nodded in agreement and settled down wearily, only to fall asleep immediately. A cold wind that followed in the wake of the twister brushed over the back of my neck, and I groaned in pain. I laid down myself and fell into a brief sleep.

Again, I had a dream that was different than the usual dreams that otherwise filled the night. In this dream, a note floated slowly to the ground. When I unfolded the note, I could decipher some curly old-fashioned handwriting:

"Follow the river; it will bring you to a large rock. From there on, follow the stars. They will lead you to a fallen oak. Look for the wisest one. Do not be afraid; I am on your side. But be careful; dangers lurk here!"

My shoulder had begun to throb again and the pain awakened me. Parilar, on the other hand, was doing splendidly when I shook him awake. I told Parilar about the dream and the incomprehensible message. But even he couldn't make rhyme or reason out of it.

We shared a meal and got ready for departure.

"What should we do now?" I asked perplexed. Musing, I looked at Parilar. I entertained doubts that the one who had sent this dream was really our friend. It could just as soon have been Gribor.

"I am leaning toward ignoring this dream. Who knows where it wants to lead us," I considered.

"I wouldn't look at it that way. Why should someone who wanted to harm us send us a message? He could otherwise just do something to us in our sleep. I suggest we follow the river and look for a sign. But we must keep our eyes open if dangers are really supposed to be lurking here."

In principle, Parilar was right. And what else were we supposed to do? So I agreed with him and swung myself onto his back. He trotted off with outspread wings. We followed the waterway that now flowed lazily through a region of flat meadows and looked for the landmarks described in the dream. The sun had just reached the middle of the sky when we arrived at a big rock. It rose pretentiously from the flat surrounding area directly in front of us and blocked our way.

"And now?"

"Follow the stars," I quoted my dream. Did we now have to wait until it was night? I looked questioningly at Parilar who looked around.

"I can't envision having to wait until night; that would simply take too long," he read my thoughts.

Suddenly, Parilar took a leap forwards so that I lost my balance, but could, however, grab on in time. I now hung onto his right side and got ready to get on his back again, which must surely have looked abundantly funny. When I had succeeded after some effort, I smirked, "I hope you had a good reason to almost throw me off your back."

"Absolutely. I found the stars!" Parilar pointed with the tip of his tail to a tree. "Look up."

I followed his order and looked up the tree. And indeed, high up on the trunk, a star twinkled.

"The stars run along there."

He pointed to other trees in which stars also twinkled.

"They are magic stars," Parilar said to me over his shoulder. "Only those for whom they are intended can see them. That means that whoever sent us the message must have magical powers, because they are not so simple to summon up. Only Zaron can do that among us, and I hope he is not here."

This sentence rattled me; I noticed my fear returning. But on the other hand, Zaron was several days' travel away, and if he had wanted to find us, he would certainly not bother with magic stars that now showed us the right way.

Indeed, we now negotiated the further journey to a giant fallen oak. But by the time we got there, it was already night and the moon stood peacefully in the sky. I only managed to keep my eyes open with effort and could no longer think clearly. We decided to first lie down to sleep and then continue to search the next day. Exhausted, I lay down.

Something blew warm air into my face and forced me to open my eyelids.

"Get up! We need to keep searching. Did you forget?" Parilar bent over me and shoved the last crust of bread that had been in the bag over to me.

"I didn't even have a chance to think of such a thing," I murmured even before getting into the food.

Parilar excused himself for a moment, as he said, and when he returned a half an hour later, I saw that he was happily licking his lips. Apparently there were wild boars in the forest.

After a sparse breakfast, I dug my memories of the dreams out of the back of my brain. Now we are supposed to look for the 'wisest one.' What was that supposed to be again? I looked around searchingly, but discovered nothing. Questioningly, I looked at Parilar, who likewise stood there at a loss and eyed the area.

"What here in the forest is the 'wisest one'?" Think. What is the oldest here?" I considered frantically. "Stones?"

"Where do you see stones here?" sighed Parilar.

Grumbling, I continued to think. What was old in forests? "Trees!"

Parilar nodded in agreement. "Now we just have to find the oldest tree."

Searching, I looked around. There were many high and thick trees around here; most of them ancient.

But after a while, I especially noticed one on the path. A giant oak at some distance stretched its gnarled branches toward the sky. We trotted off and after a few minutes, we stood in front of the ancient growth, which seemed even more gigantic up close.

115

It had already, like most of the trees here, shed its red-colored leaves. The massive roots jutted out of the soft floor of the forest like the waves of a carved ocean, so that one really needed to climb up them if one wanted to reach the trunk. I looked up the enormous tree. How was it supposed to lead us to the meeting place?

"Here." Parilar pointed to a further star at the top twinkling through the branches.

I stumbled and climbed over the roots up to the trunk, where I discovered a small hole that had certainly been carved in the tree just a few days ago; perhaps also just hours ago.

Not too conspicuous, but large enough to make me curious. I poked around in the little hollow until my fingers came upon a folded piece of paper with writing on it. This time the message was not a dream, but instead written on real paper. The handwriting was scrawled, like that of a small child. I read aloud, "You have come too late!"

The Riders

I had to read the lines again and again. What was this supposed to mean then? Someone wanted to pull our legs. Not comprehending, I looked at Parilar who was down below, restlessly bobbing up and down.

"Jella, something is wrong here!" I now heard it, too. An increasingly loud sound tore us out of our thoughts. Suddenly we discovered a herd of horses moving toward us at breakneck speed.

The horses were no bigger than ponies and carried strange little riders who were dressed all in black. Some carried swords in their hands that glinted in the sun, others held large clubs, and still others clasped halberds.

They were rapidly upon us and the horses encircled the tree with nervous little leaps. I just now saw the faces of the hunch-backed and misshapen figures.

They were trolls! In my shock, I almost fell from the root I had climbed. That was all we needed! I could hardly imagine nastier opponents here, and I was terrified. Would Parilar be able to help me? These creatures had magical powers, and I doubted whether we were up to them.

"Who are you?" Somehow I managed to not let my voice shake, although my body parts were doing exactly that.

None of the riders made any sound other than a dull grunt.

"Typical troll," went through my head. "Dumber than dirt, can hardly speak, but are sneaky."

"There comes someone else," Parilar whispered to me.

A likewise black, but this time large horse joined its fellows, and my breath caught when I recognized its rider: Gribor!

"This is certainly a pleasure. You here?" With these scornful words he looked me over, full of hate.

"What do you want?"

Gribor gave his deep-throated laugh and replied, "The rest of the Codices; you know that! Hand them over, Otherwise you will never see your friend Rose again, just as unlikely as your beloved luzo!"

His words caused a stabbing pain in my chest and I lowered my head. I had completely suppressed any thoughts of Rose in the past few days. So the thoughts of her which were now springing up affected me all the more. I lifted my head again right away. What had he just said? He wanted the Codices? But he had them, didn't he?

"I thought you had taken them back when I was unconscious."

"Don't fool around with me; tell me where the rest of the Codices are or your friend and your luzo must die,"

He gave no credence to my words. But if he didn't have them and I didn't, then who did? Zaron must have noticed them if they had lain there.

"You can't fool me. Hand them over. It will only get worse the longer you refuse to give them to me."

Seeking help, I looked at Parilar who suddenly shared over our bond, "Climb up the tree!"

I almost laughed out loud when I heard the words,

"How am I supposed to get up there; the tree is enormous!"

"You should just try to climb up there; it is simply a surprise for them. I will come to your aid as soon as I am finished with them."

I wasn't totally convinced of his plan, but I didn't have a better idea, and Gribor was becoming more and more impatient from second to second.

I sighed deeply.

"OK, I will have to give them to you; I'm in a trap," I whispered with a lowered voice to distract him.

Now my moment had come. Hastily, I turned around and wrapped my arms around the giant tree trunk. With both legs, I clung fast to it and pulled myself up, bit by bit, while my attackers, cursing, tried to stop me, for which they first needed to get off of their horses because they refused to step over the thick roots.

One of the black guys caught my pant leg, but I was able shake him off in time, before he could pull me down. Again I sensed, laughing inwardly, how much the practices on the sandy field had strengthened me.

I continued to climb and forced myself not to look down. From below I heard cries of battle. Finally I was grabbed by two enormous paws. I let go of the tree and was lifted into the air by Parilar. I laughed out loud. Once again, we had escaped from a mortal danger.

"That was a perfect plan, Parilar!"

"Yes, I am invincible," he boasted, smirking,

My arms were scraped and burned hellishly. In addition, I found myself in a very unpleasant position.

"When do you plan to land?"

Parilar didn't answer, but instead flew a tad faster and finally landed in a clearing at the edge of the forest.

"What are we doing here? This is probably the best place to be found," I scolded.

"How true. Yet this is the meeting place," Parilar explained.

"Where did you get that idea?" I asked skeptically.

"When you were still climbing and only Gribor and one of his trolls were left, Gribor bolted like the rest before him. I forced what really happened out of the fellow who was left behind: Gribor was at the oak before us and took out a message that was intended for us. He left behind the message for us that we had come too late, and as a consequence lured us into the trap. Now Gribor knows where the secret meeting place is. By the way, none of the attackers is dead. Tomorrow morning they will probably wish that they were when they feel their bruises," Parilar snarled.

He blinked at me and I felt respect for the animal. This luzo must be a devilishly strong opponent even for experienced fighters. I was happy to know he was on my side!

"How did you manage to take care of the trolls? They do have magical powers?"

"Now, I had suddenly disappeared, and then I appeared again in another spot. I simply generated a field, and every time I disappeared into the fog, I turned around right away. Because that made a few seconds difference, they never knew where I was. Thus I could always catch them individually. They didn't know the trick, so they quickly panicked."

Wow, he had thought that out cleverly. What a smart animal!

But then the memory came back to me and I shook my head. In front of us, I saw only meadow and on the horizon, I identified a big gray mountain. The forest behind us remained quiet and there was no hint of further magic signs. Where had we just landed here?

"And where has our friend gotten to?" I asked in a snippy voice.

Parilar shrugged his shoulders. "I have no idea. Maybe he'll come a bit later. Let's just rest and wait."

A reunion after a long time

We had just lain down and closed our eyes when someone stepped in front of the sun.

Irritated, I blinked and was startled at the same time; Parilar jumped up with a tremendous leap and planted himself ready for battle, the hairs on his neck bristled, only to then fall into a gentle purr. A woman with long black hair and dark brown eyes stood in front of me and smiled at me brightly. It was the woman from my dreams: my mother! Catleya!

I was speechless for a moment; my heart began to race and my feelings were on a roller coaster. I had the right feeling back then, after the conversation with Fanres. My mother was alive and I saw her standing right in front of me, and no doubt was possible, and...

"Dear Jella! I am so sorry; I wouldn't have thought that Gribor could find you. I should have been more careful."

Her voice hit me like an electric shock. I was torn back and forth. So my mother had fastened the magic stars to the trees. I still lay riveted to the spot. There stood my mother in the flesh, whom I had resented for many years both consciously and subconsciously because she had deserted me. Now I just wanted to lie in her arms, rest and cry.

I jumped up, rushed up to her and hugged her fiercely. Snuggled against her, I didn't want to ever let go of her. She placed her arms around me; her black hair blew around me like a soft curtain, and I felt tears falling onto my head.

But then she slowly let go of me and said, "It is so wonderful to see you again, my child. But now we must move on immediately. Please follow me."

"Follow? Where?" I asked uncertainly.

"To my home. I will tell you and Parilar everything, but come along quickly. Gribor could turn up here at any moment. We must now get away from here as fast as possible."

Catleya whistled with two fingers and a brown luzo came galloping up.

"That is Alaba. My truest friend in all adversity," Catleya introduced her companion, who only briefly found time to greet Parilar.

She mounted her luzo, I swung myself onto Parilar and together we trotted off.

At first I was much too excited to say anything. I had found my mother again and at this moment, nothing else mattered at all. Butterflies dashed through my stomach; I had to alternately laugh and cry and could hardly keep myself on Parilar; so great was my longing to take her in my arms, to be held by her. But the quick trot forced me to pay attention to the trail.

Soon my curiosity retuned and I began to call over to her, "Why didn't you show yourself?"

"I was afraid I would lead Gribor directly to you, because he has been looking for me for a long time. I didn't want to put you in danger because he is a brutal and dangerous opponent. But it seems that I yesterday underestimated him once again," she said in a husky voice.

A thousand other questions went through my head, but Catleya now drove Alaba forward and Parilar adjusted himself to Alaba's speed. We rode toward a huge mountain that looked even more enormous up close. The wall of gray basalt rose vertically; a foothold was nowhere to be seen.

"I think you and Parilar will be able to find my cave without problems; just follow me." We flew a roundabout way along the edge of the rock so that we couldn't be seen from below.

Catleya's home was a cave! I took a deep breath. Well, better than nothing, I said to myself. Parilar lifted off and followed Catleya's luzo. We first flew through narrow breaks in the forest, then through a low rock gateway where I needed to duck. Now we were behind the gray wall and followed a deep, steeply pitched ravine, which no human, no troll and much less a pony would ever be able to climb. Under us white waterfalls rushed, causing a boulder to tumble into the valley from time to time. Right and left, dark cliffs rose vertically to the top.

After a short flight, we came to a small outcropping in the smooth rock. Far below us stretched a huge forest; at the horizon we saw the silver band of the river that we had been following. I was not able to make out any human habitation far and wide; there were no streets to be seen either.

From up in the air and from below, the cave entrance was not visible, but when we landed on the ledge, we saw the opening a few meters below us. It was hidden behind a spiky protuberance.

"This is where you live?" I asked when Catleya had joined us. Alaba remained in front of the cave entrance and Parilar joined her.

We must have been very high up because it was already becoming noticeably cold even though it was only afternoon. So we retreated into the cave.

Alaba got a blanket which she would hardly need because she, like Parilar, had a thick winter coat.

I wrinkled my nose, because what would happen if it now began to snow? One would freeze here! Did Catleya really feel comfortable in such accommodations?

"Yes, I like it here. But I only live here during the summer. In the winter, I prefer houses down in the forest. Even though I often have to flee from Gribor there," she said with lowered eyes.

Had she read my thoughts? I must have looked scared because she suddenly roared with laughter.

"Naturally, that is part of my gift," she said and looked lovingly at me. "The same as you are able to do with Parilar."

On the one hand, I found that exciting, but on the other hand? Did I need to beware of her now?

She laughed again, took me in her arms and said, "No, I can also turn it off; think what you want to think; I don't receive what doesn't concern me anyway."

Whew...That was plenty complicated. Well, I thought, the main thing is I found her again. I felt tears rise in my eyes once again.

"That means that you have watched me all these years then?"

She nodded, bit her lip and now I saw that big tears were rolling down her cheeks, too. "Yes, I often sought contact to you through dreams, but in order to not place you in danger, I never spoke to you."

I went to her and put my arms around her. "But why didn't you simply live in Hokksund and take me with you? And why did you give me away to that terrible family anyway?" It bubbled out of me.

"You will learn all of that, but first make yourself comfortable." She pointed to a bed, and I sat down, thankful for the opportunity to be able to rest.

"Are you hungry?" she asked. "I can cook something for us."

"Oh, yes. That would be great!"

122

Soon Catleya handed me a bowl of soup and sat next to me on the bed while I ate. The warm broth did me good, and I felt better right away. When I had consumed a second bowl, a warm glow came over me.

"Would you like to now find out, what happened?" Catleya asked and cleared away the dishes.

I nodded eagerly and sat up in suspense.

"Well, when your father died..."

"I saw that in my dreams! He was murdered by Gribor!" I interrupted her.

A wave of grief cast a pall on her face. "I know; I sent you the dreams. The time had come for you to know the truth. Even if it was only in dreams."

Surprised, I paused for a moment. Catleya had sent me the dreams?

Promptly, Fanres' words shot into my memory. Catleya's talent was controlling dreams! Why hadn't I thought of that before? Now everything made sense!

"My talent is controlling dreams," she repeated my thoughts.

"I showed you the images of how Gribor prevailed. Yet before and after that, so much more happened."

She continued, "When we - the Great Five - were chosen, we were proud and wanted to become the best generation of all times. Your father Adrian and I soon fell in love with one another. No one had a problem with that except-"

"Gribor!" I interjected.

"-exactly, he loved me, too, and was jealous of your father. Gribor wanted to get rid of him, but if he were to do that, he would at the same time destroy the Great Five. So he thought out a plan: He wanted to make it look like Adrian stole part of the Codices and as a consequence, he would have been banned automatically, and someone new would step into his spot.

"But to his misfortune, I saw through his plan and Adrian and I lay in wait for him and we deterred him. We wanted to remain the Great Five, and so he agreed to keep his attack on us a secret.

"We no longer spoke of the incident and after some time, we believed that he was completely one of us again. Soon afterwards, Gribor lived together with another luzo rider and had a small son with her.

"Until then we thought he had come to terms with his destiny and Adrian's relationship with me; but one day he ambushed Adrian and me.

He threatened us: Either we separate or we should disappear forever. That meant he wanted to kill us.

"He was power-hungry and hate-filled. But we didn't pay enough attention to his words. We believed that when he had accepted that we belonged together, he would at least ignore us, but we had erred horribly.

"One day he murdered Adrian after he had lured him into an ambush. I was desperate and hid because he now wanted the Codices and then me. He had become crazy, completely berserk, and was just ranting.

"Gribor wanted to snatch the holy books, to achieve absolute power. There were luzos in another part of our world who were not kindly disposed toward us, and he wanted to join with them and bring our village and the country under his rule.

"Before he could steal them, I got possession of part of the Codices and fled. It was only a small part of the first book that I took with me, but it was one of the most important.

"The first part of the Codices is namely essential, because all of the crucial knowledge about luzos is found there. And anyone with this complete knowledge becomes invincible, because he is master of the luzos and their magical powers.

"So I fled with my luzo. I didn't want to end up like Adrian, or have to be at Gribor's service, and besides, I didn't want to lose you. I was pregnant with you at this point in time." My mother smiled dreamily and stroked my hair.

"Yet I had once again underestimated Gribor. He followed me and managed to kill my beloved luzo and seize for himself the part of the Codices that I had rescued.

"Gribor, on the other hand, had misjudged my capabilities; I secretly followed him after that for days. One day, I succeeded in taking the books from him as he slept. I sent him a few nice dreams. With this trick, I got them from him again and brought them to safety.

"There was still a further part of the Codices. It was the part that your father transformed into this silver circle on your neck before his death. Because Adrian had the talent to change things. And after Gribor's first attempt to separate us, Beleia advised us to hide this part as a precaution. She suspected something at the time.

124

"Gribor knew nothing about it; he desperately continued to search for the part that would bring him complete power. But your father had transformed it.

"Even if he had found it, the pendant would have been useless to him; he would have needed to find someone who could change it back." She pointed to the silver pendant that dangled around my neck.

Wide-eyed, I looked at her.

"You mean I had the missing part of the Codices with me the whole time? Why didn't you tell me that before? I could have taken it back to Tyrsenor long ago."

"That would have been premature. No one would have believed you and if you had told them that you got it from me, their prejudices would have been confirmed. Everyone suspected Adrian and me of having stolen the Codices. And besides, someone must first be able to change this pendant back again."

I nodded in agreement. She was right about that. No one would believe us. Zaron had locked me up and hadn't even given me the chance to prove my innocence. But who could retrieve the holy books of Tyrsenor from the silver ring on the golden chain around my neck so that I could appease Zaron?

"After that, I was constantly on the run from him. When with Beleia's help, you finally came into the world in a hiding place, I was afraid he would take you from me also.

"Beleia was the only one who knew about me and my secret. Her talent was to make things appear and disappear or also to be able to make invisible and to heal. She had seen through Gribor from the beginning and had never trusted him. Unfortunately, she couldn't bear the shock of the betrayal, because she is very sensitive. She withdrew to the woods with her luzo and lived alone. She didn't want to have anything to do with all of that anymore."

With his luzo, Gribor had more chance of tracking us down that I did without a companion! So I decided to follow Beleia's advice and give you to a family in the other world, a world that Gribor did not yet know. It had to be a family who would be easy to bribe and consequently didn't need any papers for you. And who also had something to do with luzos. I had enough gold; Beleia had provided me with that from the mountains.

"Adrian's luzo was the only one in that generation that knew the way over there and with him I left Tyrsenor.

The Capuchs were very useful to me. Their ancestors formerly lived in Tyrsenor, but had to leave the village after some strange incidents. Or rather they wanted to live among the people outside and enjoy luxury.

"At any rate, that was what I knew about them, but I didn't know the real reason for their rejection of the village community, and I also didn't know how they managed to get through the wall of fog. But that had already happened many years ago, long before my time.

"In spite of their rejection of our community, Beleia revealed to me that they were obligated to us. I have never found out the reason for that either. This family has always remained a puzzle to me.

"Beleia cast a spell over the pendant and the chain before we sent it with you. To us, it seemed to be the safest with you. She made it invisible and you never noticed it all those years. Only a short time ago did Beleia release the magic, and I sent you the dream that turned the responsibility for this part of the Codices over to you.

"When I had given you away, I flew back and then further to the north, here, which no one from Tyrsenor knows, erasing the trail to you.

"I would have liked to have stayed together with Beleia, but she lives near our home and that was too dangerous for me.

"In my thoughts, I was always with you and was in contact with you through dreams and thoughts. Even if you never saw me, I always watched over you.

"Unfortunately, Adrian's luzo died soon after that; he never got over losing his rider.

Too late, I noticed that he also missed the energy from Lake Landuza, which our luzos urgently need from time to time.

"During my escape, I fortunately met Alaba. She belongs to a clan of luzos that live her in the lowlands. Her family doesn't know Tyrsenor and she had never before seen a human wither. But she felt drawn to me even though we don't have a bond with another, and so she stayed with me.

"Unfortunately, a few years ago, Gribor also found a luzo who had once found the way into the other world a long time ago. He disastrously belongs to those who are unkindly disposed to us. And so he was able to take up the trail to you a while ago, using you to find me. He then lived over there a long time and befriended a policeman named Louis Taperzo, for whom he went stealing, which was easy for him because he could make himself invisible for a period of time."

"Louis is a criminal?" I asked interjected, startled.

"Yes, in his greed, he banded together with Gribor, and they stole whatever they could get hold of. The strange Chief Inspector sat in his office when Gribor invisibly appeared again somewhere and stole. He then handed the loot over to Louis. In exchange, the policeman then provided him with information and expedited the search for you.

"I lured him onto false trails a few times with dreams, but eventually he picked up your tracks with your strange computers.

"Since he can make himself invisible, he recently succeeded in following you using his contact with the police, and so found the way back to the village, too, because his luzo didn't know the way back from the other world and always ended up in the wrong time period. Every luzo only has one pathway at its disposal; it cannot change to another time. That's how everything had progressed then and now the events are starting to happen very fast.

"A few days ago I had visions in which I saw how Gribor came back. I saw him in a cave together with the Codices. And then I observed a blurry murder.

"I was greatly alarmed when I sensed that because I thought you were in grave danger. No one knew about the cave and the secret passageway; that was my secret. That was true at least for a while, until Gribor once invisibly followed me.

"Therefore I set off for Tyrsenor in the night, in spite of the threat that Zaron presented for me there. To not be conspicuous, I had to send my luzo back to the lowlands when I reached the edge of the area, because the other luzos would have sensed her as an unfamiliar creature.

"During the same night I lay in wait, although I had no idea how I would be able to help you. Then you came with Lesla.

"Gribor knew the cave and the tunnel to the room with the Codices because I was once careless, and he had followed me that time. And so he tried to seize the other part of the books. When you followed Gribor with Lesla, I tried to protect Lesla but I reacted too late.

"I was also very afraid of Gribor. Sometimes when I expend a lot of energy, I can create visions during a waking state. I sent him a vision – as I said, unfortunately too late – and momentarily confused him. So for a moment, he couldn't remember where he had put the Codices.

"When Gribor then disappeared, and you fell unconscious, I snatched the other part of the Codices before he could find them again. I didn't want to surrender them to Zaron either, because I feared that he would blame you for stealing them."

"Which he then also did," I then muttered to myself in a grim voice.

"They were the books that Gribor pilfered earlier," continued Catleya.

"With which I fled because Zaron had already advanced into the cave with a group of luzos. Gribor was so afraid of Zaron that he simply left the Codices behind."

I stopped breathing when Catleya stood up and came back with the silver sheets from a corner in the unlit part of the cave.

"These are the introductory parts. But they are completely useless on their own because they only derive meaning with the section of the book that Adrian transformed into the pendant on your neck.

"I knew that Zaron would take care of you because he is very responsible. Since he had always suspected me of stealing the Codices, I wanted to continue to avoid him. Then I secretly followed him when he took you along. In the end, I waited until you got out of the cell.

"I already planned to break in myself to rescue you. But I didn't have to since a nice young man freed you.

"I then temporarily hid again with Beleia. She trusts me greatly and because of that, she gave me her luzo a few days ago so I could come after you. Having arrived here, I sent back her luzo and with Alaba, I began to mark the way, laying a trail for Parilar, and then observed your quest. I got the magic stars from Beleia.

"Luzos have a difficult time here in this area because their powers fade here so far away from Lake Landuza.

"I rode behind you and when I had found you in the night with Alaba's help, I sent you the dreams. Together, so I thought, we could conquer

Gribor and bring back the now complete Codices to their original place, but I had no idea that Gribor had companions..."

"Catleya," I interrupted her. "This nice young man of whom you spoke earlier is Lacato, Gribor's son."

She stopped short and raised her head in surprise.

"Hmm...apparently his son is not malicious. His wife was an endearing person at any rate, who just didn't recognize her husband's lack of character."

"What's even more important: Gribor kidnapped my best friend."

"Rose?" asked my mother in return, her eyes opened wide.

I nodded awkwardly. "You know her?"

"Yes, I saw you together often in my dreams; that is truly atrocious," answered Catleya. The color of her face had now turned ashen.

"Gribor told me that I will see Rose again when I give him the Codices. Do you think we can talk to him and hand over the Codices to him in exchange for Rose?"

I cringed when my mother answered in a hard voice, "You can forget that. Gribor would take the Codices from you, laugh scornfully and disappear. He is completely insane and would have fun torturing you. I fear that he would then kill you as a witness.

"No, we must think of something else. No question that we have to free Rose; we will do that. But not by Gribor's rules."

I breathed deeply. I didn't recognize my mother so full of hate, and after the gentle conversation before, it had the effect of a cold shower.

She appeared to have noticed that because she now put her arms around me and consoled me, "Jella, in all the years on the run, I have become too hardened. Please pardon me; I should have said that more gently. But Gribor is too dangerous. We will free Rose; I promise you that. We will track him down, and in the critical moment, we will think of something to outwit him."

She kissed my forehead gently and I huddled against her. We were silent for a while. I needed time to process all this information. Parilar could surely help us.

"If my mother has been on the run from Gribor all this time, we must put an end to him," I discussed with Parilar through our bond so that no one else could hear; apparently, that included my mother, too.

Parilar, who had already come into the cave with Alaba a while ago, had listened to my mother just as intently as I had. He signaled me his agreement.

"Catleya, we'll both help you to conquer Gribor," I declared.

The search ends and a hunt begins

During the night we shared the only bed, which was no more than a blanket on a pile of straw.

The warm glow that emanated from my mother soothed me. How often had I imagined this! Longed for my mother! And now I lay next to her and heard her regular breathing in the silence.

We had spoken with one another for many more hours and then I had fallen asleep. I had much to tell her, about my adoptive family, about Rose, school, the Capuch grandparents and ... During the night I woke up once and watched her sleeping for a while. How similar we looked!

"Good morning, Jella!" The soft voice of my mother awakened me. I sat up half asleep and yawned extensively. Against my will, I threw back the blanket and stretched my numb limbs.

Outside, haze still hung over the meadows and forests and reminded me that it was almost winter already. Parilar and Alaba still slumbered in front of the cave. I crept as quietly as possible to Catleya who kneeled in front of the cooking area.

"I'll make us tea. I have other provisions there, take a look." She pointed to a crate.

I rummaged around between bread, vegetables and cheese, when Catleya suddenly asked me, "What is actually your talent?"

"I didn't receive it before Lesla died."

Catleya laughed quietly and replied, "Everyone carries his talent from birth, however, usually first notices it when it is needed."

"Hmm...Maybe it's different for me. I don't have the faintest idea what it could be."

I then decided upon bread and cheese and sat down next to my mother. Parilar could go hunting for himself up here on the mountain and take Alaba with him.

"So, what are we going to do now? Where do you think we are most likely to find Gribor?" I asked after our meal.

"First you need to rest, Today, you have the whole day for yourself and Parilar. Explore the area and look for signs of the trolls. In the process, you

131

can recover a little because the coming days will surely be demanding. When it is dark, we will discuss our strategy. Agreed?"

I nodded eagerly.

"Ready?" I asked after breakfast and winked encouragingly at my luzo who was whipping his tail back and forth adventurously.

We had flown down to the meadows at the foot of the mountain, moving along the edge of the rocks where trees still grew. In doing so, we avoided being seen by a distant observer.

Parilar absolutely wanted to run; this way he could more easily find the trail of the trolls than from the air.

Down there it was still warm; the winter had not yet completely set in and the low sun promised a warm fall day.

"Can't you run faster? You're running like a slowpoke!" I teased.

We already had put a good distance behind us, yet I wanted more speed. It was glorious to run with Parilar over the open meadows. His soft paws flew noiselessly over the dew-moistened grass, and I could feel every one of his muscles. We stepped it up a notch until Parilar stopped, panting.

The ride had now tired me, too. But it had been really fun to simply romp about. Groaning, we lay in the grass and wheezed in competition. We had forgotten the trolls since Parilar was not able to pick up a scent at the beginning. The wet grass cooled of our heated bodies delightfully, and I closed my eyes in enjoyment.

Suddenly a mild gust of wind blew over us and dried my sweaty face. I sensed how this little gust of wind gave us new strength and right away felt like a new woman. We needed that!

"Wow! One would need to experience that kind of invigorating little breeze more often," Parilar marveled.

I was still too dazed. How could we have recuperated so fast? Now I wanted to fly. A moment ago ground work, and now up in the air! Lithely, Parilar stretched out his enormous wings and started off. Together we defied gravity and I felt infinitely happy. I could linger in this moment forever, but logically, that was impossible.

"Up for a few loop-the loops?"

Aghast, I opened my eyes wide.

"Don't you dare! I'm warning you..."

I didn't get any further because Parilar had already begun to turn on his own axis. I swallowed my vicious scolding as Parilar completed a double loop-the-loop.

We had hashed this out weeks ago already! Flight exercises and all kinds of clowning around in the air, but no loop-the-loops! Never in a million years! Desperately I clung to his neck and prayed that this ride from hell would soon be over.

When Parilar's wing strokes had calmed. and we were gliding steadily through the air, I started right in again.

"You....dumb...stupid...cat thingamabob!" No better insult occurred to me. "This will have consequences," I ended my helpless lecture.

But instead of apologizing or even regretting his decision, Parilar burst out laughing.

I crossed my arms, snorting with rage, but regretted it right away when Parilar, distracted by laughter flew into a small air pocket that luzos are normally able to locate quite well.

"Are you almost finished?" I asked when his attack of laughter lasted over a minute. Slowly, Parilar breathed in and out until it appeared that he had himself under control again.

"'scuse me, I will control myself. Promise! But-"

"No but," I quickly objected. Under no circumstances did I ever want to experience something like that again! If I had known that cats could be so silly, then, yes then, yes...no matter.

We slowly flew back at a low altitude. On the way back, we tried to get an impression of the terrain and scout out possible paths that Gribor could have taken.

On the following day, I awoke on my own. Today, we would find out where Gribor was located. In the evening, we had also found the first clues, like trampled grass, and planned our route.

A faint uneasiness came over me, an emerging fear? But I also felt anticipation, along the lines of hunting fever. Or had Parilar infected me?

Outside, a fine sleet passed by, making the meadows and countryside further below appear gray in its drizzle. It was nasty cold weather, and for the first time this fall, I wished for the summer.

133

I woke up several times during the night, because an unchecked storm outside gave its power full rein. In the course of this, I briefly felt a desire to fly with Parilar in the clouds. But then his hijinks of today came to mind again.

After a meager breakfast we moved together down the mountain and rode carefully near the forest on the edge of which we found the trail the day before. If felt a bit uneasy; I feared a renewed encounter with Gribor, but under no circumstances did I now want to show any weakness. Upon arriving at the edge of the forest, the fine drizzle turned into a strong downpour. The cold drops pelted my face and the cold felt like sharp needles being stuck into my skin.

"Come, we'll enter the woods a ways; it will provide us protection from the rain." With these words Catleya slipped in between the trees.

My clothes stuck to my skin as I followed her.

"Where do you think Gribor is staying?"

Catleya turned to Parilar who was at that moment curling back his lips so that one could see his pointed teeth.

He lifted his head, sucked in air through his large nostrils and got scent of something.

"To the east! The trolls stink quite strongly, and their odor trail is already a day old. Soon it will have disappeared."

Tediously, we stalked several hours through the underbrush, high rock walls moved closer and closer to the left and the right until an old fallen linden tree blocked our way.

"If we go around the gorge, we will lose too much time," my mother concluded.

"Parilar, how did Gribor get around it?"

"He didn't have to go around it at all. The tree probably fell over after he came along here. I can be of help to us," the luzo said.

He lifted his paw and slit open the trunk like a knife in butter. Groaning, the old wood yielded and already after a few minutes, Parilar had cut open a passable path for us.

I was astonished; I had again discovered abilities in the animal for which I hadn't given him credit. With this thought, it became abruptly clear that I had viewed Parilar as an animal up to now. He looked like an animal, moved like one and I hadn't given any thought to the fact that his behavior differed so much from that of humans and animals alike that I now became aware that I would have to learn to judge him differently. But there was no time for that now.

The path now became so narrow that we had to reassuringly encourage Alaba to finally forge ahead through the narrow rocky path, where she was just as wedged in on the left and right as Parilar. It now went steeply down the mountain, and suddenly, we stood in front of the entrance to a low cave. Even the ponies and trolls would surely have gotten through here only with difficulty. On the tips of my toes I crept forward and peeked around every corner. After a few minutes of noiseless creeping we became accustomed to the twilight. Soon it became lighter; we had come upon no obstacle and the cave exit lay before us. The trolls and also Gribor must have felt very safe because otherwise, we would have certainly come upon guards. We entered deeper and deeper into the forest, when our path suddenly ended at a thorny thicket.

Carefully I pushed a few branches apart and peered through. The gap provided a sight that stopped my breath. In the middle of the forest, behind a protective wall of an impenetrable hedge of thorns, was a huge camp of simple huts and tents. The surrounding rock walls towered so high that their peaks disappeared in gray banks of clouds. A tempestuous stream of wind moved through the ravine behind us and moved the tips of the massive fir trees on the rocks so that it looked as if giants were fighting.

Hundreds of trolls milled around or did work, which consisted of shoeing horses, sharpening weapons or erecting new huts.

In the middle of the camp was a single white tent, and out of it stepped precisely the man we were looking for.

It was Gribor and at his sight, I cringed intensely. Cold chills chased over my back, and fear gripped me so powerfully that I trembled violently. In spite of that, I succeeded in keeping my head, and I tried to get an idea of the camp.

But why hadn't we detected this camp earlier on account of its noise? A gust of wind cleared up my question. We had tailwinds! Hissing, I drew in air and let the branches glide into their normal position, In a whisper, I told my companions what I had just discovered.

"What are we going to do now?" Questioning, I looked at my mother who had turned pale.

"Never in my life would I have expected Gribor to acquire so many allies. I suggest that we sit tight until the wind turns in our favor. Then we can eavesdrop on them and perhaps glean some useful information."

I nodded in agreement and pushed a few branches apart again. If theses damned gusts would just turn!

All at once, I heard voices. It was trolls who communicated with another, more like grunting than speaking. Aghast, I looked over my shoulder and tried to get a view of the two people whose voices I heard. But I saw no one apart from my two companions.

Amazed, I moistened my finger with spit and held it up. Indeed, the wind had all of a sudden turned and I could hear the voices of the ugly creatures who were fiercely fighting in the camp.

"That is all pointless! We can attack tomorrow, too! Why all this hanging around?"

This voice belonged to a stocky troll with a pug nose and gray hair that almost reached to the ground. He stood in front of a fat little crony whose hooked nose almost touched his chin it was so long. Well, then he could at least smell his own bad breath.

Both wore sleeveless vests of greasy brown leather; their tight pants were tucked into bucket top boots, and their shapeless fat stomachs were entwined with a wide belt, without which they would probably have burst and from which short swords dangled.

Placatingly, the one insistently talked (or better grunted) to the other, "If we attack in three days, our armor and weapons will not be ready yet; Without them, we will have no chance against the luzos. Because then we would have to head out right away. For that reason, this change in plans was resolved. Until then, everything should be ready. As it is, we need three or four more days until we reach the village, if not longer. So, go back to work!"

Snorting, the long-haired one turned on his heels and joined a group of disgusting dwarves who were sharpening swords together.

My gaze wandered further to Gribor standing at the fire, greedily stuffing himself with pieces of meat. He looked in the direction of where the small head troll still stood.

"Jacal, did you give everyone the word?" Gribor inquired.

"Yes, sir. All have been told, even though not everyone was satisfied with it." The last part he said more for himself, yet Gribor stared at him.

"What satisfied? Does everyone believe this is an amusement park here or what? We have a plan to head out in three days at the latest to attack the damned city of the luzos! And don't babble at me full of this nonsense again!"

Snorting with rage, Gribor strutted away, leaving the intimidated troll behind.

Now I knew what they intended. Gribor planned to attack Tyrsenor. He wanted to take the Codices with force. I had seen and heard enough.

I gave my companions a hand signal to follow me without a sound. When we had left the ravine and could speak to another again, I immediately stopped.

"Gribor wants to attack us! In just three days they want to march off; we must do something..." I gasped.

No matter what, we had to think of something to warn Zaron and the village!

When we had been silent for what seemed forever, Catleya began to speak, "Good, we'll go to Tyrsenor and inform them ourselves. Regardless of how dangerous that might be for us. We can and must save hundreds of lives. We'll set off right now!"

I hesitated. Did Catleya really want to risk her life to save the village? We were no longer wanted there; the residents hated us, and the danger of being killed by them when we showed up again was high.

Nevertheless, it was my community! Despite the animosity of the residents of Tyrsenor: I wanted to likewise risk my life. Better for me to die than the whole village!

Silent and brooding, we ran the way back for many hours. At the edge of the forest, I swung myself onto Parilar with a grimly determined face and was about to give him the signal to take off, but my mother stopped me.

"Jella, Alaba is not so fast. She doesn't have the energy from Lake Landuza and is rapidly exhausted. Fly ahead, I'll come after you as fast as I can."

Thoughtfully, I mulled it over. A spark of hope spread through me. Could Parilar carry two people? I sent the question silently to Parilar, who led me to understand that he would at least give it a try.

"Come with me, Parilar is going to try to carry both of us," I explained to Catleya, who at first stared at me in disbelief. Something flashed in her eyes. She liked the idea.

"Alaba will find her way back to the cave of her family alone; she knows her way around here better than I do."

Lovingly, she stroked Alaba's neck and whispered something into her ear. The luzo was already trotting away. Not without first giving Parilar a gentle nudge with her nose in parting.

Quick as a flash, my mother climbed onto Parilar behind me.

"How did you manage that?" I asked impressed.

"Years of practice," she laughed.

Zaron's mistake

The dawn softly caressed us; the first rays of light were already spreading. We had flown the whole night and felt hungry and exhausted.

Parilar had done well and carried us far. But now the beating of his wings also became more irregular, and we landed to recuperate and eat something.

I lay in the grass and rested. A stubborn thrush landed on my stomach and chirped her morning song. Reluctantly, I sat up after a while. The thrush hopped up with a start, looked at me reproachfully with her black eyes and flitted off.

From now on we went on foot, because Parilar was too exhausted to continue flying. The next hours and days only crept by, but they passed, and we came closer and closer to the village. Since we had flown the first stretch, we had surely gotten a big lead on the trolls with their small ponies. But Catleya and I now also felt that the hurried march had cost us much energy. We were moving slower.

The day we wanted to warn the village dawned with a cold gray sunrise. This morning, there were huge storms, and we had to brace ourselves against staggering gusts of wind to make any progress. The wind beat against us so brutally that I stumbled several times. As if it wanted to keep us from our goal! Soon I was so exhausted that I sank groaning to the ground. This damned wind should change direction already, so that we would have a tailwind.

"Jella, what is wrong?" My mother and Parilar turned and came toward me.

"I can't go any further, the wind is too strong!" Within minutes of speaking these words, the wind began to turn and give us a tailwind, much to my boundless amazement.

"It appears the wind has had a change of heart. Come, we are almost at our goal."

We accelerated our steps and progressed quickly with the tailwind. Soon after, a wall of clouds appeared and for a while we stumbled through wet gray wisps that the wind drove ahead of us.

The forest now took on a familiar shape; the beech and chestnut trees that had accompanied us the past few days gave way to sturdy old oaks.

We climbed over a rock wall and beyond it, began our descent to the plain on which the village was located. The mist dissipated, and we left the wind, too, behind the wall of rock.

Soon enough, I recognized the shape of the towers of the settlement and in that moment, I would have liked to have been able to kiss the ground in relief. According to my calculations we had arrived in time, and by the next day, half the village could already be prepared for battle, if not even all of it.

Arriving at the edge of the village, we met the first early risers who had set off this morning to get firewood for their stoves.

As soon as they recognized me, they uttered a scream and ran back into the village. Shortly afterwards, a threatening group of villagers came thundering toward us. Zaron led the men who were carrying clubs and swords.

Parilar planted himself in front of us snarling; his fur bristled and he bared his white teeth.

"What in the name of the devil are you doing here? After you fled from the prison, we looked for you to take back the Codices."

Zaron scrutinized us angrily. It was only too apparent that he and his people would have preferred to behead us immediately.

Only Parilar held them in check. Why didn't they call their luzos to help?

I defied his piercing eyes and explained in a quiet voice, "Listen and don't interrupt me! We did not steal them! Gribor had the Codices. Catleya, Parilar and I discovered that he has formed an army of trolls to attack you. We have come to warn you. You must clear out immediately or arm yourselves to fight for your village!"

Zaron studied me in disbelief until his gaze caught Catleya.

"Catleya, number two of the next to the last generation."

He looked at me briefly. "The most recent generation no longer exists since Lesla was murdered, and Jella was identified as the murderer. I should have known I would set eyes on you again."

Catleya smiled coldly.

"Yes, I hadn't intended to let myself be damned here again, since you declared me the thief of the Codices. I am thoroughly offended! But I told the truth; you must acknowledge that you lied to yourselves, because you didn't want to think. I had no reason to steal! And you would have

140

discovered that with a bit of logic, but you wanted to confirm your damned prejudices.

"I feared that Gribor would have stolen them before me, and then you would have been subjects of a power-hungry crazy man! But none of you wanted to admit that you had misjudged Gribor! And now you are also accusing my daughter of murdering Lesla, although you would only have to think to realize that it can't have been her."

She literally spat out the last words.

"What did you just say? Jella is your daughter?" Zaron stuttered with an expression of disbelief.

"Yes, she is my daughter and the child of Adrian. And therefore she belongs here."

In the meantime, more villagers assembled behind the group of men under Zaron's lead and eyed the scene warily. A woman with dark green eyes suddenly screamed out in rage.

It was Gribor's wife and Lacato's mother!

"Catleya, I don't think that now is the appropriate time to be fighting with us here! That is ancient history; that was your generation. The Great Five no longer exists; no one else received a talent." The latter she said turned to me.

"No, the Great Five is not yet over! I have figured out Jella's talent, although she has not yet discovered it herself."

Baffled, I looked at my mother. What was she claiming just then?

Zaron's eyes opened wide. "What was that you said?"

Catleya nodded thoughtfully. "Yes, Parilar can confirm it, too, isn't it so?"

I fixed my eyes on Parilar. How were he and my mother supposed to know what my talent was and I myself didn't?

"Yes, I have observed it for a some time now. She controls the wind and the storm!" he boomed.

I turned pale and gasped for air; What was Parilar claiming there?

"Don't joke around, Parilar!" Zaron looked at him punitively. He didn't believe a word.

Parilar snarled loudly. He bared his teeth again and whipped his tail. Apparently, he had lost his respect for Zaron.

Zaron slid back a step and now summoned several riders together with their luzos. To my horror, they closed in on Parilar. First the riders on their backs had to expend an astonishingly large amount of effort the hold their luzos in check. They were springing to and fro like crazy, and some of the riders didn't succeed in staying on their backs. It looked chaotic and ridiculous, to see the riders trying to force their luzos in our direction, only to have them move back as if there were an invisible wall.

Later I learned the reason for this confusion from Parilar. Luzos were bound to their riders in absolute obedience. Their ancestors had taken this vow a long time ago. But they were also linked to one another and stuck together unconditionally.

Parilar sent a subconscious message to all luzos close to him that we had come to save the village and had important information to share. And so most of the luzos felt more connected to him than their riders and had considerable difficulty remaining loyal to their masters. I didn't learn that until later; the confusion now and the wildly determined faces of the riders were frightening me.

The riders soon controlled their luzos, and the lingering exceptions only slightly reduced the number of fighters.

Seeking help, I looked into the crowd and viewed a face that was so trusted for me. I would preferred to have cheered at his sight: Fanres!

Heavy-hearted, he looked at me and raised his hand. I hesitantly waved back and felt deep warmth. Someone was on our side.

The riders crowded closer and closer around Parilar, Catleya and me. They forced us in the direction of the building in which we had been imprisoned just a short time ago.

It felt like a punch in the stomach when I comprehended what they intended to do with us. They wanted to lock us up again and not fight against Gribor. They simply didn't believe us.

Trembling with rage and fear, I closed my eyes and wished that someone would come to our aid.

Suddenly I felt a breath of air. Wind! If what Parilar and Catleya claimed were true, then wouldn't I have the ability to command the winds to somehow help us? It was worth a try. I started to inwardly summon the wind. I imagined how the storm would raise the dust on the ground around me, push the riders back and knock over Zaron and his men. And so I began to sink deep inside myself and feel myself a part of the storm. No, as master of the storm.

But only a little breeze arose and cooled my heated face. Downcast, I let my hands fall and surrendered. This didn't make any sense at all.

But suddenly small grains of sand swirled and rose above us. Thick dark clouds all of a sudden raced across the sky; lightning struck nearby and spilt apart an oak. A storm approached and swept around our heads.

No, it raged around Zaron's head and the heads of the people standing across from us; it whirled up the sand and swept it into the riders' faces.

A smile stole its way to my lips, and I felt new power rising within me. I whirled around to Parilar and swung myself onto his back. The sky had darkened, and huge cumulus clouds loomed on the dark gray horizon.

Now I sensed how I could direct the wind. I conducted the rising wind under Parilar, and it carried him into the air. He floated without effort over the gathering.

I steered the vortex of the storm over Zaron and his companions. I made their luzos scatter with a hard gust of wind.

From above, provided that the people who had gathered in such great numbers were still standing or sitting, we could see mirrored in their faces the astonishment and horror caused by these forces.

Zaron and most of his companions soon lay face down on the sandy ground and held their hands protectively over their heads. At this moment I commanded the eddies to flare up a last time and then to die down. Then first one, then two, and finally three luzo riders with their luzos rose up to join me.

They wanted to show me that they believed me! Now we were ready to fight against Gribor!

I commanded the wind to continue to calm and wait and see.

Still uncertain about my newly-learned abilities, I was amazed that the storm actually subsided right away. Small eddies still flew over the dry ground and covered Zaron and his companions with little piles of sand, but then that, too, was over.

We landed again and I dismounted. I now stood between Catleya and Parilar. The brief storm had left us completely untouched.

In front of us, in the dust some meters away, Zaron and his cohorts stood up and shook the sand from their clothes. But Zaron still had this stubborn look as if nothing had happened.

"Enough now, we will bring you to the dungeon," he snarled angrily.

Now I had had enough. I flew into such a rage that I could no longer stop myself.

OK, he was the leader of the village; he had the responsibility for everyone, but now this had all gone too far. He would bring everyone into danger with his stubbornness and allow Gribor to become the most powerful person in the country. Only because this Zaron imagined he had to force through his will! In normal times that was probably right, but now it was totally inappropriate. And all that, just because he didn't trust us.

Later I would probably have allowed myself the pleasure of sending him a small, well-proportioned tornado again. But I was not yet completely aware of my power, and my wrath simply turned off my mind. So I shouted at him with all the energy at my disposal, "Damn it all, don't you understand anything? Does one have to smack you with a sword for you to take note that the whole village, the luzos, everything is in danger? Wake up already! Gribor is on the way here with hundreds of the vilest thugs, armed to the teeth! He wants to destroy everything here, and you want to lock up the only ones who can help you! Wake up already and get to work! We must arm ourselves for battle!"

My fists were in such tight balls that my knuckles turned white, my chin jutted forward, and I must have looked like a fury because Catleya and Parilar, yes, even this cat, looked sideways at me, aghast.

That was, I later became aware, the height of disrespect, and when I remembered it weeks later, a belated queasy feeling still rose in my stomach.

But Zaron still didn't want to believe me. For him, loyalty to a former member of the Great Five counted more than the arguments of a stranger, which I had been to him a short time ago.

"Gribor belonged to the five riders and was a part of us. He would never do anything to us and..."

That was the last straw. With raised fists I made a dash at him and screamed, my voice cracking , "Do you sometimes also think? Gribor drove Catleya away; he killed my father; he also killed Lesla in front of my eyes. Do you believe he would stop short of killing you? He wouldn't even stop at his wife and son!"

Now I heard a scream again. It came from Lacato's mother. She stood leaning on her son, quivering; both held one another in their arms. Both of them were ashen.

"How can you say such a thing? Gribor is Lacato's father; he would never hurt us," she screeched, distraught.

Zaron nodded slowly and donned his self-opinionated look again.

I became nearly crazy as a new wave of wrath washed over me. If Zaron were to open his mouth now, I would scratch out his eyes!

Instead, Lacato spoke and we could hear him even though he stood several meters from us. It abruptly became quiet as his voice rose, "Jella is right. Gribor once told me that he will come back. He never wanted to be my father; he admitted that was a mistake. He wanted Catleya to be his wife and never got over her having chosen Adrian. I was, he said this, the reason for the marriage to you, and he bitterly regretted it. We mean nothing to him."

This last sentence he addressed to his mother. Tears streamed down his face, and he held onto his mother, who now also broke out in tears. She had known it; she had known from the beginning, and she hadn't been able to hold onto Gribor even when she had become pregnant. Her dreams and wishes dissolved into nothing on this square, on this morning.

Now Zaron opened his mouth again, "Yes, but..."

At the same moment, one of his fellow fighters stepped up to him and whispered something into his ear. He spoke quietly, but not quietly enough, so that I could also hear it.

"Zaron, call it quits," the tall man, to whom a gray beard lent a certain dignity, surely making him a natural leader among Zaron's companions. "There has been enough talk, enough 'yes, but,' enough quibbling. If you don't yield to reason on the spot, we will withdraw our allegiance from you. You will sit down together with Jella and Catleya and deliberate what is to be done."

Zaron's face suddenly resembled a cleaning rag that had just been wrung out: He looked gray and wrinkled. Apparently, he comprehended what was at stake and recognized that he had become obsessed with a false notion. His illusions shattered.

145

But now and in the subsequent hours, it became apparent why he had been chosen as leader in his time: His dream world burst and collapsed in on itself. He had hoped to be able to arrange everything without too much effort and in his own way. But this dream was over.

Now he had the greatness to accept his mistake. He could sense, as he admitted to me much later, that he had suppressed his feelings of warning. By repressing all conflicts and dangers, he saved himself the trouble of thinking and let himself in for flights of fancy. It was his mistake, and he would make good for it.

He led and carried the responsibility; he knew his abilities, and he knew that the villagers trusted him. He decided to correct his mistake and to provide for the survival of the village.

Because that was what it was about now: about life and death; no more and no less.

To thwart large, existential dangers, one had chosen and trained the Great Five with the help of the luzos and the knowledge of the ancestors. They were the core of the protection for the village.

Lauren and Fedor positioned themselves next to Parilar already during the fight with Zaron. We were three and so there was already a core that could help Tyrsenor.

Lesla was dead because she had tried to protect me. So only four of the Great Five were left. That would surely weaken the defense, but it might perhaps be adequate, even if the ritual 'five' was not fulfilled. Gribor's son Lacato also belonged to the Great Five. How would he react?

I looked over to Lacato. He still had tear-stained eyes and his face was pale and haggard.

When I looked at him, he looked up and his appearance changed. His facial expression became rigid; he narrowed his lips and looked at me with his clear eyes, "I belong to the village and the Great Five. My task is here," he spoke loudly across the whole square.

His mother looked up, surprised, but then she gave him a kiss on the face and said something to him.

He came to us. We were four again. It could work!

Battle at Lake Landuza

The rest of the day passed by with deliberation and initial preparations before I permitted myself a little sleep, which was mixed with uneasy dreams.

Zaron had come to the conclusion that Lesla's appointment must have been a mistake and that the final member of the Great Five had to be chosen immediately. But that could not happen fast enough before the anticipated attack; a luzo sensing a bond with humans had not been identified.

The next morning, I looked at my wristwatch. It was purely mechanical, without bells and whistles, and therefore, it had continued to work the whole time.

Today was November 26th, a Monday. At least in Hokksund. Actually I would have needed to get ready for school at this time, but that idea alone appeared completely foolish to me. Besides, I had already missed so many days that it now didn't matter.

There were more important things. For example, saving the village and fighting against Gribor.

Most of the warriors had already arrived at the big square. Dozens of swords and armaments were being repaired and adapted. The houses were equipped with protection against fire. A baby cried pitifully and a consoling voice tried to calm it.

Why did all this have to happen? The idea went through my head with a touch of grief.

"Hello, wind girl!" I turned around. Lacato!

A smile played on his lips and a wave of joy washed over me.

"That was really a remarkable feat yesterday. I wish I also knew what my talent is."

"My mother says that each of us carries his talent from birth... although I had no clue at all beforehand."

"I also don't have the foggiest notion what mine could be."

We didn't talk to one another for a few seconds that suddenly stretched into an eternity. In his presence I felt strange; something in my stomach became totally soft, and all of a sudden, I saw myself as weak and helpless.

147

Catleya came to my assistance. "Well, you two. Everyone is working, but you are lazily standing around here!" she teased.

"Then I'll look for where help is needed..." Lacato turned on his heel and went off.

My mother chuckled impudently and punched me in the side. Then her smile died.

"Jella, I must ask something of you. You must go to Lake Landuza and moisten your necklace with a drop of the water. The Codices must be complete again. In their true form, I mean. Because otherwise they have no power, and we will become weaker.

Fanres told me that you have the ability to approach the spring. So you are the only one in this generation who can enter the holy grove. I am certain that this is the legacy of your father.

"The water of the spring alone should be sufficient to produce the old form again; that's how your father planned it. In addition, you should bring back a larger quantity of water. The trolls have surely brought along some magical objects, and we don't have enough Landuza water to neutralize them. It would be best of you were to fly off right this moment."

"But the battle...," I began.

"I have spoken with Zaron. You should hurry and fly off right away. You will make it back in time. We urgently need the water and the Codices here before the battle begins. Your battle clothes are already in Lesla's old house. But go now, hurry!"

I nodded. So be it, if even Zaron commanded it! Since he exercised his leadership role again, my respect for him had returned and so I obeyed.

It took some time until Parilar landed at Lake Landuza. The sea lay there reassuringly still. The grove around the columns emanated peace, and a deep longing came over me. I let myself down on the shore and again sensed the attraction of the water. How I would have liked to dip my head under! I fell into temptation...

The lake was so overwhelmingly beautiful. Slowly, I began to lower my head to the turquoise water when I was suddenly pulled back.

I turned around and looked angrily into Parilar's face.

"What are you thinking?" I snapped at him indignantly.

"Jella, you dare not put your head in. Only a little with your hand; Fanres explained that to us the last time! That is dangerous. Think about it; we don't have forever!"

Enraged, I grumbled to myself and unfastened the golden band from around my neck. I felt a difference right away. Now that I no longer wore the gold chain around my neck, nothing drew me to the water any more. Was it the pendant in which the Codices were imprisoned, which absolutely wanted to take on their true form again?

Slowly I dipped two fingertips into the cool liquid and moistened the pendant with a drop of Landuza water.

I didn't think I could trust my eyes, because what I now saw was beyond unreal! The circular pendant that still lay in my hands, melted instantly into a thin, rolled-up surface that took on the form of the Codices. Now I held the first part of the Codices in my hands! So now they were complete!

They looked a bit different than in my dreams. I had anticipated holding parchment in my hands. Instead, I found a large number of square plates, engraved with long sentences in the strange handwriting that I had already seen on the column during my initiation.

The plates were just as light as they were pliable; I could roll them without having the writing change. Normal sheet metal would have surely buckled under the treatment that I gave the documents. Every other metal known to me would have been less stable. The weight was also not greater than that of a normal book a few hundred pages thick.

That's how the plates were joined: On one side they were tacked together or fused so that one could leaf through them like a book.

Greatly pleased, I looked over the individual pages, but couldn't locate one familiar letter. Laughing, I stood up and was just about to go to the grove to fill the leather pouch I carried on my back with water, when I became aware of a sound.

Parilar and I froze momentarily. All at once, it was deathly quiet. A rustling of underbrush that was pushed apart and a cracking branch broke the silence. What could that be?

Trembling, I turned around. My face froze to ice when I discovered the giant paws of a luzo, then the huge body, almost twice as large as Parilar's, then his sharp, bared canine teeth and his enormous wings. His fur was just as light as Parilar's, but it shone with a dull bluish cast.

I cried out quietly when Gribor stepped out from behind him.

"WWhat ddo you wwant hhere?" I stuttered.

He burst out in derisive laughter and pointed to my left hand, which held the Codices so tightly that my knuckles bulged.

"I knew that I would find you here. Zaron never has enough water from this spot in his house. His father, who was the high priest in our time, taught him that. So he had to send out someone who could endure the energy here, to be remotely able to fight against the trolls.

"I wanted to prevent that. That I've meanwhile been delivered you and the Codices at the same time makes matters considerably easier.
Then I won't need to pick up my stinking buddies any longer."

Threateningly, he stepped toward me, and I almost lost consciousness when his repulsive stench addled my senses. With outspread fingers, he stretched for the valuable documents, and I disgustedly breathed in his musty odor.

"Never!" I breathed and stumbled back another step.

Snarling, his powerful luzo came toward Parilar, who stared back defiantly.

In my thoughts I sent Parilar a giant doomed question mark.

"Do what?"

The answer came right away, "Scram."

"One, two, three!" At 'three,' I jumped onto his back and Parilar shot up.

A cry of rage resonated from Gribor's mouth, and I couldn't suppress an amused chuckle.

"Don't you look fool-" I couldn't finish my sentence because behind us, Gribor and his luzo headed purposely toward us.

My malicious pleasure gave way to a rising panic and I clung tighter to Parilar's neck. The Codices burned my body like glowing iron but I forced myself to think.

I quickly stuck them into my shoulder bag. What were we supposed to do now? Gribor would catch up. Slowly but surely! It would be better to face one's opponent than to flee! In the long run, we would not hold up forever and then we would be more exhausted than ever.

"Turn!" I shouted to Parilar.

Gribor's luzo barely managed to avoid us when we performed a daring braking maneuver. His luzo first dropped several yards, but then rapidly caught himself. They hadn't counted on that.

At first, Gribor looked baffled; then a nasty grin appeared on his distorted face. He caught up and both of them fell into flight next to us.

"Smart girl. Now give it here!" Gribor stretched out his hand to me.

As if I would indeed hand over the Codices to him, I drew closer to his outstretched hand and grabbed it as fast as lightening to turn it with a jerk in his direction when he pulled on the Codices.

Also a surprise maneuver that Sagor had taught me. Instead of exercising resistance, one pushes quickly in the intended direction of one's opponent and gives him a strong push. That surprises almost everyone.

He lost his grip and had to clamp onto his luzo with both hands, meaning that he could no longer grab the Codices. With an outcry, he almost fell from his luzo, but at the last minute he clung to the thick fur of his animal.

"Okay, as you wish!" He bared his teeth and pulled himself up again.

Parilar flew away under them and around them. That confused Gribor's luzo, so that he paused for a moment, and I took advantage of the chance to give Gribor a kick.

He had apparently not practiced already for a long time. That gave me confidence, because if he remained so rigid, his strength would be of no use to him against our dexterity.

Our opponent snorted in rage and drove his luzo with hard kicks in his side. He followed us with powerful beats of his wings.

Suddenly, Parilar roared in rage. Gribor's beast had bitten his tail! With flashing eyes, Parilar whirled around and bit the wing of the shining blue monster. It screeched in shock and dug its claws into Parilar's stomach, who paid him pack by sinking his teeth into its shoulder.

Both animals turned around one another and I had to hold on tight to Parilar's body to not slide off of him, because both luzos twirled around one another like a giant ball of fur made of wings, claws and teeth. That disrupted my plans, because I had actually wanted to avoid a direct battle, which we could only lose.

Filled with hate, Gribor's eyes flashed at me and in a new tack, he grabbed my long hair. I screamed out and had to let go of Parilar's back with tears in

151

my eyes. The pain shot through my body, hard and brutal, and made me motionless. Gribor pulled me roughly to him and tore the Codices from me. Then he let go.

I had lost. Like a rock, I fell through the air and looked almost unconcerned at the quickly approaching ground.

I loved the feeling of flying and I loved the wind softly caressing my cheeks. I closed my eyes. I was floating! Gently, I glided across the huge Lake Landuza and broke through the glassy surface with my fingers.

But what was happening now? The downwind carried me gently to the shore, and I stood with both feet on the ground! Right away, gravity made itself known, and my trembling knees caved in under my weight.

For a short time I had forgotten everything, surrendered myself to weightlessness and enjoyed floating with the wind. The wind rescued me! As crazy as that sounded, it was also true.

A gust of wind caught me and carried me safely to the ground. The wind obeyed me at the moment when I imagined floating gently to the ground.

Like a stabbing pain, everything returned to my consciousness, Parilar! Where was he? Searching, I looked up to the sky and spied the furious bundle of fur.

Gribor tried with all his might to free his luzo from Parilar; he had what he wanted! But his white giant fought so bitterly with Parilar that he paid no further attention to his rider.

"Parilar, let go; we are defeated. Gribor already has the Codices!"

His half-choked answer came without delay. "Never! Send the storm to help you and let it give you power. Then we will continue to fight! We're not giving up so fast!"

So it was not over yet. I took a deep breath and made an effort. With a vigorous movement I called the wind, and it hurried to help me, Next I commanded a strong squall to Parilar. And now it was my turn: My next command created a funnel cloud that lifted me high above the fighting animals.

Furious, I pulled myself onto Parilar's back. With a hard shove, Parilar broke loose from the other luzo, which was pulled up by another whirlwind.

Now I sent a blast of wind to Gribor that lifted him from his seat. In a wild panic, he opened his eyes wide. Parilar hastened toward him, and I ripped the book out of his hands again.

Gribor was much too surprised to react. He was surrounded by the wind, caught in a funnel cloud!

"Go, fly away!" I ordered Parilar, and we took advantage of the tailwind.

The storm gave me renewed strength. But all of a sudden, I felt an invisible border between the wind and me. I apparently could not take too much and I couldn't command it too much; the use of my talent was only limited.

So I flinched hard when I heard the beat of wings behind us and turned around, horrified. The storm had abated, and Gribor's luzo had picked up his rider again. They were battle-ready. again

Oh, no! It was still not over. Why did Gribor have to be so tough?

"Fly! Fly faster; he's coming back!"

Parilar panted beneath me, and I realized that his injuries were making it hard for him. What would I do if he died? Gribor's luzo was much stronger than Parilar. It was less seriously wounded than my loyal companion, and we couldn't continue flying forever. They would catch up to us and seize the Codices!

But I was one of the Great Five! Our task consisted of guarding the Codices! I had to defeat them!

Immediately a vast abyss opened up under us. In the depths of the ravine, a silver band glistened, a river that reflected the morning sun. My stomach tightened when I sensed that Parilar was becoming weaker and weaker and hardly had enough strength to stay in the air.

"Will you make it over the abyss? You must try, please!"

I shuddered at the sight of the rocky cliffs. I could not look down and scrunched up my eyes. Fearfully, I looked around once again and dismayed, realized that Gribor's luzo was flying directly behind us and was just opening its mouth wide to grab Parilar again.

Parilar evaded. With an extremely skillful loop-the-loop. He had only faked his weakness to entice the other luzo into a careless attack!

Then he hit Gribor's luzo hard on the shoulder with his paw. This blow fell accurately and was forceful enough to tear off a wing of the opposing luzo. My luzo was clearly more skilled, cleverer and nimbler than the other animal and that compensated for its strength!

The loop-the-loop had unleashed panic in me again, but this time I was nevertheless delighted that Parilar had practiced it. In the future he could do as many loop-the-loops as he wanted.

Only a small bloody stub still held the right wing of the animal that almost rolled over right away. With a gruesome scream, the monster fell down into the darkness of the rocky gorge.

But Gribor had reacted fast enough and had grabbed onto Parilar's left hind leg when the animals collided. With an iron grip, he held on. Looking over my shoulder, I saw his eyes. They were the eyes of a madman, wide open and full of hate.

He dangled on Parilar's hind leg, and it made it difficult for Parilar to continue flying. My opponent almost had lost hold for a moment; it appeared that he would follow his luzo into the depths.

"How could Gribor let his luzo fall into the gorge alone?" I asked myself, shocked. "What kind of a rider does such a thing?" Again, I understood that Gribor was ice cold.

He managed to pull himself halfway up onto Parilar's hindquarters, who was now near exhaustion and only laboriously balanced the too heavy weight on his back. We rapidly sank into the gorge, rocky cliffs passed by to the right and left of us.

Parilar no longer had enough strength to keep his altitude. We sank deeper and deeper toward the river. Everything went as if in slow motion. Probably only a short time had passed since the beginning of the battle, but it appeared to me as if the conflict had lasted the whole day.

Greedily, Gribor's hands groped for the Codices; he had indeed managed to get on the back of the cat. He could grab the bottom part of the Codices. The book tore into two pieces with an ugly rip.

But now everything went quite fast. Though I had previously been unfocused and at the end of my strength a short while ago, this sound pulled me out of my growing exhaustion.

Crazed with rage, I took hold of the other part caught in Gribor's hand with a lightning-fast movement and struck his head with a well-aimed kick. The kickboxing training was yielding its first results!

Completely surprised by the speed as well as the force of the kick, he lost hold for a moment.

I quickly braced myself with both hands on Parilar's back and used my heel to give my enemy another kick in the head. A roundhouse kick – I had heard the name once at a boxing meet in Drammen and had told Sagor the name when he showed it to me.

That finished off Gribor. With a horrible scream, he now let go of Parilar. When he fell into the depths, I saw his piercing eyes, which were wide open in panic!

Skill overpowers strength!

After a few seconds of free fall, Gribor struck the river. I saw his body plunge into the foamy white water in a cloud of spray. Shortly afterwards, he seemed to be pulleded along by a waterfall and disappeared.

Parilar managed to twist himself up, and during the bumpy flight, I looked over his shoulder down into the depths to observe whether Gribor appeared again.

Only now did it occur to me that Gribor was the only one who knew where Rose was. He had kidnapped her and wanted to use her as a hostage. The battle had consumed all of my energy, and I now would have given anything to save Gribor, if I had thought about that during the altercation.

Parilar's battle

Parilar was completely exhausted. He still managed to get just to the edge of the gorge; then I flopped off of his back and he fell non-stop onto his side. We had both run out of steam, and I briefly lost consciousness. I didn't wake up until a velvety snout caressed my face.

Parilar!

Trembling, I stood up and looked at Parilar's body, dotted with numerous wounds. He had been back on his feet first and let me rest a while longer.

Tears rose to my eyes and I felt more miserable than ever.

"Parilar!" I rasped. He snorted and softly laid his head in my lap. Sadly, I stroked his cheek until my gaze fell upon the torn documents.

The Codices!

Breathing hard, I sucked in the evening air. I had let the torn Codices lying here. Oh, no! How could everything have come this far? Weren't the books were made out of nearly indestructible material? What power had torn them apart?

Rose! Like a punch in the stomach, the knowledge returned that Gribor had taken the secret of Rose's hiding place with him into the abyss.

Distressed, I looked into the sky. I crawled on all fours to the edge of the cliff and searched for a sign of life from Gribor. Perhaps he had survived the fall! If we were able to get him alive, we could somehow pump the secret out of him!

In the battle, I had acquired several painful injuries which I only now really began to feel. But my fear for my friend and my sorrow let the severe pain fade into the background. The thoughts circled in my head: How could I find Rose again? And how could I save Parilar?

I had no idea where we were and how we were supposed to survive the coming hours when I heard a rustling: the beating of wings!

Panic-stricken, I turned around like a flash, ready to fight right away again. Could Gribor's luzo have escaped from the gorge and now wanted to seek revenge on us once more?

But then I recognized a familiar silhouette and my heart took a joyful leap. It was Jali, and Lesla sat on her! But then I remembered that Lesla was dead, killed in front of my eyes by that traitor Gribor.

156

Immediately I felt a deep pain when reality struck me again. Lesla was irrefutably dead! I was mistaken. Had let myself be lulled by my wishes. My eyes needed a moment to recognize the rider. It was Catleya! She had adopted Jali as her luzo!

She didn't let Jali completely land before already jumping off, running to me and taking me into her comforting arms.

"Jella, my dearest! Oh, no. How could I have sent you off alone? Are you all right?" With tears in her eyes, my mother looked at me in concern. She had been crying. She took my face into both hands and then moved them gently over my hair.

I only said, "Catleya," and snuggled into her protective arms again.

"Gribor lay in wait for us at Lake Landuza and then attacked us." I gulped at the memory.

"We managed to shake them off and let them fall into the gorge. Oh, God, we killed them! And he took the secret of Rose's hiding place with him to his death."

All the blood drained from my face. Only now did I notice that Gribor's death and that of his luzo caused me to have deep feelings of guilt, above all, because I now wasn't able to help Rose any longer.

"That is not your fault, darling. It just happened; no one is blaming you for his death. He attacked us and you, and so he brought his death upon himself. Furthermore he murdered your father and Lesla. It is good that everything is now over!"

Lovingly, she stroked my hair and then looked at Parilar. Her eyes widened at his appearance and she rushed to him. Hissing, Catleya exhaled and stroked Parilar's injuries with one hand.

"This doesn't look good. Jella, we urgently need water from the lake; The trolls have attacked us much sooner than we thought. The only reason we haven't lost yet is because Gribor, in his greed, left them shortly after the beginning of the battle. Give me the leather pouch; I will quickly fly to Lake Landuza and get water from the holy area."

I was deeply shocked; I had completely forgotten the army of trolls.

"Will you be able to handle the energy at the lake?" I asked out of breath when the situation became clear to me.

"No, you are right; I would fall into a trance and not get away without help. Do you know what? Take Jali and fly there quickly. Bring as much water with you as you can carry and come back to us. I will stay here with Parilar in the meantime."

No sooner said than done. I hopped on Jali's back, which was considerably narrower than Parilar's. Then I directed her away from the abyss in the direction of the holy area at the lake.

I dismounted at a bit of a distance since I didn't know what effect the mist would have on Jali, and I had no desire to have to go back on foot with a luzo that had fallen into a trance. At the edge of the spring, I kneeled down and filled the leather pouch with the holy water. As quickly as possible, we rushed back to Catleya and Parilar.

My luzo had rolled over on his side. He lay in a deep faint when we arrived. I was distraught; under no circumstances did I want to lose a friend. Parilar had become part of me. We formed an inner union, so that I didn't know how I would get along without him. I sank to my knees beside him and began to sob.

Catleya laid her hand on my shoulder and squeezed it. "Jella, perhaps you can help Parilar. Some of the chosen also have powers of healing. Since you are the only one in this generation who can touch the holy water without falling into a state of intoxication, it could be that you can also use the healing power of the water. Zaron told me that you had visions at the holy grove; he was deeply impressed by that. In our generation, it was Beleia who had this power. She was our healer. Please try to cure Parilar with the water; it is our only chance."

"You mean the water can save my luzo?" I asked in return, through a veil of tears.

"If you also possess the power to heal, then that will be possible. I'm slowly beginning to believe that you may be one who possesses more than one ability within yourself. According to Zaron, it only happens once every twelve generations that one of the Great Five is endowed with several magic characteristics. But we will only know if we have tried."

"What do I have to do to save Parilar?" I hastily asked.

"I often watched Beleia when she healed injuries. She took water from the holy area of the lake, drizzled it on the wounds and recited a healing saying from the Codices."

I cringed. Drizzling water over Parilar was easy, but what healing saying was I supposed to recite? Nothing would come of this.

I noticed how the rage was rising in me. I carried the water with me. The Codices were in my hand. At least part of them. Parilar lay in front of me and would die if I didn't help him. Suddenly, lightening flashed through my head. I opened the pouch of water.

"Wait, Jella," cried my mother quickly. She grabbed Jali and moved back several yards.

Out of the pouch rose a strange scent. It smelled like myrrh and lavender mixed with a undefinable aroma that reminded me of something familiar. But I couldn't say what it was.

When I had sniffed it a little, my perception changed. All at once I saw waves of color hovering over Parilar.

There were black gaps in these whirling patterns where his wounds were located. Then I saw a deep black gap in one wave, under which there was no wound. Without thinking, I realized that here was where the most serious injury was. It was deep inside; evidently the kicks and bites of Gribor's luzo had damaged inner organs. These colored patterns indicated the way for me.

With a fast movement, I poured some of the clear liquid into my hand and drizzled it into Parilar's open mouth, which I quickly closed again while holding his head up high. He now swallowed hard and I felt that he had ingested the water. After that, I treated the visible wounds from the outside.

But nothing happened.

"Of course, the healing saying," I spoke to myself, disappointed.

My last hope was now the Codices. If Beleia had her incantation out of the book, then contact with the book would have to help, too!

So I took the thin pages in my hand and wiped them over the pattern of waves. The black spots disappeared where the book reached them. I was relieved! Finally something had worked!

Only the large internal injury continued to show a black gap in the colored waves. In my renewed dismay, I now drizzled some of the elixir on his stomach and placed a further dose in the luzo's mouth. Then I instinctively unfolded the pages and pressed them against the moist spot that lay under the black hole in the colored pattern.

Parilar's body began to vibrate. The pattern slowly changed. Next the black changed to a deep blue that became lighter and lighter, then went through red to a light yellow and finally glowed white.

I jumped back terrified when Parilar suddenly uttered a loud scream.

"Do you want to burn me? That was much too much." He screeched indignantly and jumped up as if bitten by a snake.

My mouth gaped open out of fright and amazement. I had probably given him too much water. But now it appeared that my luzo was on his feet again and felt a powerful thirst. With a single bound, he was in the air and shot down into the gorge with a few powerful wing strokes.

At first I believed I had made a terrible mistake, but when I looked over the edge of the gorge on my stomach, pale and trembling, I saw Parilar floating below over the waterfall, taking in tremendous amounts of liquid.

I looked around and saw Jali and Catleya who watched with wide-open eyes and held her hands in front of her mouth upset.

I called to her, "Everything is in order; Parilar is just drinking; it seems that he is very thirsty."

Then I jumped up and wanted to run to both of them and hug them.

My mother held her hands defensively in front of herself, "The pouch, close the pouch!" she shouted in warning.

Oh, I had completely forgotten that. Others appeared unable to bear the vapors of the holy water.

Soon after we fell into one another's arms laughing in relief when Parilar appeared over the edge of the gorge, his stomach swollen with river water, in a bad mood, but healthy.

The attack

Catleya interrupted the scene with hasty words, "Quickly now, we must hurry to get to the village. Who knows what has happened there in the meantime."

We dashed off without further words. We could find explanations for the healing later. On the back of Parilar, who now appeared to be completely recovered, worried thoughts gripped me, and I strongly hoped that we were not arriving too late.

Already far from Tyrsenor, we saw pillars of smoke rising and we soon also recognized luzo riders, who shot through the air with violent movements. So everything was not lost; the battle was still going on.

But why were the luzos flying so high and not intervening from above as we had practiced? Not long after, I understood why the luzos could not intervene in the battle.

"The trolls are shooting with fireballs," Catleya shouted excitedly to me through the noise of battle that now droned up to us.

"Those are magic bullets that float at a predetermined altitude and can follow opponents."

With them, they held the luzos at a distance.

We had now arrived over the battlefield and preliminarily circled at a safe altitude to get an overview, still far above our own luzo riders who couldn't see us because they were looking down, of course.

Under us a gruesome sight presented itself. My three comrades-in-arms and other luzos could only helplessly watch the battle under them. None of the Great Five except me had discovered his talent yet, and therefore we were not any more useful than any other luzo rider. All were held at a distance.

The trolls had shot fire into some of the wooden houses of the village and besieged the stairs to the archives, which the fighters under Zaron's leadership had barricaded with beams and rocks.

My stomach clenched; from above, it looked completely hopeless.

Several hundred of the hideous gnomes hacked at the wood of the barricades with axes and halberds and tried to advance, while others piled up rocks on the back side of the building. They apparently wanted to build a path to the platform of the archives and attack the defenders from behind.

161

A third group constantly shot fireballs at the luzos floating above to hinder them from coming to the aid of their friends on the ground.

"Trolls are actually much too stupid to come up with such ideas on their own. Gribor must have worked with them on this strategy for a long time. In the end, he felt so sure of himself that he allowed them to proceed alone," Catleya shouted to me through the noise of battle.

I looked at her briefly and began to think. A direct attack with the luzos was impossible; the fireballs were too dangerous for that. How could we intervene without putting the luzos in danger?

"How about a little wind?" I heard Parilar growl, who appeared to be bursting with impatience and rage.

"Hmm, I can send a storm, but now I know that I must budget my powers. And I can't really steer the wind yet; it could also go wrong. If we unleash a storm, then it is not clear that it wouldn't harm Zaron's group in the archives. How would it be with a little straight wind to collect the fireballs and let them rain down on the trolls?"

"Sounds good, just start and don't babble any longer," grumbled Parilar. Was he ever angry!

I focused, closed my eyes and waited a moment. Then I inwardly saw a vision, how a wind came up, oriented itself to one point on the ground and pulled away all the fireballs at the backs of the trolls who were in front of the barricade. That would have to do for now.

When I opened my eyes, I raised my hand and showed the wind the way.

At first nothing happened. The wind seemed to need a while to be able to concentrate its movement. Finally I saw eddies arise at the edge of the sandy area, rising up quickly.

The eddies collected themselves under us, but over the other luzo riders. Somehow I appeared to have made a mistake.

Catleya and I now soared down and shouted to the other riders that they should make a hasty retreat. They just now noticed us because they had been looking down the whole time and tried to find a gap in the wall of burning bullets. But they quickly understood and raced off to the side before the cloud of dust could engulf them.

Jali and Parilar shot up again vertically and I tried to direct the storm to let the bullets rain on the attackers. That was more difficult than I had imagined. I would probably have to practice this for a long time. So it cost me a great deal of effort to adjust the wind again and again. But finally it worked.

In their furious rage, the trolls hadn't even noticed what was brewing above them. The layer of floating fireballs moved in the dust eddies that I had mistakenly conjured up instead of the straight winds, slowly down and then these round torches all of a sudden fell down on their launchers.

An indescribable chaos ensued. Hundreds of misshapen trolls raced away screaming, the hair of some burned, others literally had smoking boots.

This shift had come so suddenly that they didn't understand what was happening to them at all.

Their ponies were the first to race away; those who rampaged at the barricade ran screeching after them in a wild panic. In the space of a short time, they were driven away and scampered up the slopes to the forest as fast as they could.

The groups of luzo riders recognized their chance, and filled with rage, they raced after the stinking, smoking mob.

Parilar, too, wanted to let out his immeasurable wrath on the pack, but to his great annoyance, I commanded him to land on the platform.

The trolls on the back side of the archive continued to build. These beings are not only utterly stupid, but are also so stubborn that at no point of time do they think about what is taking place around them. The fireballs were gone; their comrades had fled in a wild panic, and they were still hauling rocks.

I couldn't, however, send a storm any longer. I had already lost much of my energy in the fight with Gribor and in my last, almost failed attempt to dispel the trolls, the rest had been used up. Now we had to choose another tactic, and therefore, I wanted to have Parilar on the platform.

Having arrived below, I jumped off and ran to Zaron who gave a completely exhausted impression just like the other fighters.

"Finally you come; we had already given up on you," he snarled. Apparently, he didn't realize who had chased the trolls. I was indignant at first.

Evidently my facial expression had not escaped him. His forehead smoothed a little and with a voice that sounded friendly for those who knew him, but to a stranger would appear an insult, he said, "Thank you for the storm; if it hadn't come at the right time, things would look bad for us now."

I was baffled. He was and remained an old diehard, and it must have cost him greatly to thank me. All the same, he had nicely acknowledged my and Parilar's contribution to the rescue.

"Zaron, let's not lose any time," I said in a tone of voice that was supposed to imitate his unfriendliness.

"Behind the tower, the last remaining trolls are building a wall and want to attack us from the back side. We must do something."

"Did you bring the Landuza water and the Codices?" he returned without responding to my tone, which would have surely been a provocation for him under normal circumstances.

I nodded and handed him the leather pouch and the Codices. When Zaron noticed that they were torn, he turned pale.

"Only the luzo of a magician is capable of that," he grumbled. "No other creature is capable of this. How did this happen?"

I described in as few words as possible my battle with Gribor at Lake Landuza and he listened intently.

"So, so," was all that I heard from him afterwards.

"Everyone, listen here," he then called in an imperious voice into the group.

"We now have Landuza water, and I will at this time hold the ceremony that otherwise takes place before a battle. We will soon have a battle because the next horde of trolls is waiting to attack us behind the archives," he informed the astonished group.

Zaron stepped to the portal of the archives and commanded that the beams in front of it be removed. Then he went through the opened portal into the foyer and laid the Codices on a pedestal.

"Warton and Heron, you guard the books until we can bring them safely into the center while we prepare for the battle," he commanded two young fighters from the group.

Later, I learned that these two were his sons. Then he turned around and had the portals locked and secured again.

Together, we all stepped over the destroyed barricades down into the village to the platform that was used for ceremonies.

Far away behind the dark archives building, we heard the clamoring trolls, who were still unaware of the changes.

But it was clear that we wouldn't be able to win any battle against them without additional energy. In their rage, our luzo riders had unthinkingly raced after the already dispersed trolls. We saw them far up in the mountains where they dove down again and again. I noticed Parilar's longing look; he would have liked to join in the battle.

"Wait a little while, my tomcat," I teased him somewhat mischievously. "There are still enough left and soon you will really be able to have your fill." Now I felt my own pent-up rage and thirst for revenge looking for an outlet.

No time remained for a further exchange of words; Zaron had begun with the ceremony. How hurried he was, could be seen by not first putting on his ceremonial clothing. He led the ritual in his battle uniform.

First he poured the water in the bowl in front of the column; then he held his hands over it and murmured a few sentences. Individually, every fighter had to step forward. Zaron took a few drops and drizzled them carefully into the mouth of each one. He spread water over every weapon that was held out to him. I positioned myself at the end of the line. When I stood in front of him, he looked into my eyes, startled, and hesitated. Then he contained himself and I, too, received my ration of the holy water. Apparently he still didn't think me capable of fighting for the village.

I sensed right away how I was changing. A powerful energy went through me; all fatigue was blown away; I only wanted to fight!

It was high time. The first trolls appeared at the back side of the platform and sniffed to and fro, searching for humans.

Zaron divided us into two groups. One was supposed to go around to the back of the archive building and attack the trolls from the back side; the other group was supposed to recapture the platform and drive the attackers back over their ramp. That's what happened.

With one exception. Parilar and I were the only luzo team remaining in the village. Catleya and Jali and the other three of the former Great Five had taken part in the pursuit of the largest horde of trolls and had disappeared behind the mountains.

So now we climbed up alone, because we wanted to carry out the attack from above. I had taken a small club for myself that one of the trolls had left lying on the square, although I knew that I was no good in direct battle.

With a loud roar of rage, we entered the fray. The first group around Zaron had stormed the steps to the archives and beaten back the wildly fighting trolls on the platform.

The second group had not yet reached the back side, although they were underway at a run.

Now Parilar stepped in. In a nose dive, he shot toward the enraged trolls who were striking out around themselves, and with each attack, he grabbed one of the trolls and let them drop next to the archives.

I didn't trust my eyes when I saw these creatures turn into rocks upon impact!

The second group reached the back side of the archives and drove the trolls forward. With a terrible wail, they were trampled, and everywhere one of the swords hit an intruder, he turned into a rock. I was completely perplexed and didn't understand what was happening at all.

It only took a few minutes for even the last troll to disappear, and only a pile of gray boulders in the strangest forms lay on the plateau in front of the huge building.

Parilar landed carefully and when I looked around, I asked him, "How is it that the trolls turned into stones? Aren't they living things?"

"I don't know either," he murmured in a dark voice.

"Something is fishy about this matter; let's ask Zaron."

With a grim face, he stood on the parapet and was just commanding some fellow fighters to search the area for fugitive enemies. When he saw us, his face lit up for a brief moment. But in no time, he was his usual self again.

"That was a magnificent battle," he condescended to hint at his feelings.

"Why did the trolls turn into rocks when we touched them?" Parilar now asked.

Zaron's expression darkened, "There are beings that return to their original form when touched by the holy water. Here it means that these trolls were formerly rocks from a faraway area that we avoid because enemy powers rule there. Only a powerful magician can awaken them and bring forth trolls

166

from the rocks. It fits with the tearing of the Codices. For that, too, formidable magic is required.

"Gribor must have found a powerful magician who helped him to attack us. We must be careful, because that has not happened for a long time now, and I had believed that we wouldn't hear of anything like that anymore.

"Only the Codices report about him in one location and warn about his power. The spot is ancient; our people had not even arrived here yet.

"Also, only rock trolls are capable of dealing with fireballs. The others that you chased with the storm were a group of forest trolls from the northern highlands who normally stay out of our way and are peaceful, as far as that is possible for such gnomes.

"Someone must have prepared them quite purposefully and skillfully, because the stupid creatures would never come up with the idea of attacking others on their own."

"What will happen with them," I asked, concerned. "Will the pursuers kill them?"

"By no means. They are like cats and have seven or even more lives. I hope that our people give them a proper thrashing and chase them over the mountains. They will have recovered by tomorrow; trolls are extremely tough. It is only important to chase them far enough away so that they don't find their way back to us again. Their memory doesn't hold more than a few days, and if they're in the forest once again, this here will be forgotten to them."

I was relieved, because in spite of the great danger in which we had been, I didn't want any carnage. Far over the high peaks of the mountains, I now saw the group of luzo riders coming nearer. They floated in slowly; one could see that the luzos were exhausted. Their eyes and those of the riders flashed wild and proud when they came closer, and I knew right away that they had been successful. Without saying much, the pairs withdrew and the fighters took care of their carriers.

A few hours later the foot troops also came back. Only Catleya and Jali were still missing when we lit a large fire in the darkness. Everyone talked at once and told about how they had driven the trolls back into the forest they had just left several days before.

The ponies had ultimately thrown off their riders and likewise taken back their freedom, because they had been caught by Gribor's troops especially for this campaign.

I asked the riders whether they had seen Catleya and Jali. No one could remember having sighted them in the air.

I was tired; the wounds that I had gotten at Lake Landuza hurt and I felt that I was losing more and more strength. The worries about Catleya who had not yet appeared masked my pain.

Zaron had guards posted and I crept past them to the edge of the valley to see whether Catleya or Jali were anywhere to be seen. For hours and hours, I stood there and looked longingly and full of concern in the direction of the mountains where my mother had disappeared.

When a waning Saturn indicated the arrival of early morning and the celebratory fire far below me burned out, I saw a dark contour rapidly approaching against the gray of the brightening horizon. It was a luzo and it carried – Catleya.

Relieved, I sank to my knees, buried my face in the morning dew and began to cry uncontrollably. Shortly thereafter, my mother, Jali and Parilar, who sensed where I was, came and picked me up. When I caught sight of my mother, healthy and with rosy cheeks from exertion, I knew that I could let go. Everything went black before my eyes and I fell in a faint.

Convalescence

Bathed in sweat, I awoke from uneasy dreams and wiped the sleep from my eyes. A dully flickering little candle cloaked my room in a yellow light and lent it a little coziness.

I took a deep breath and got up from my soft warm blanket. Right away, I became dizzy, and I had to hold on to the back of the chair for several seconds.

When I could more or less stay on my feet again, I pulled on a sweater and padded barefoot across the cold stone hallway. I remembered that I had lain here for several days and nights already, visited only now and then by my mother, who brought me food and drinks. I was much too worn out to observe anything else.

Now I was somewhat fit again and longed for Parilar.

They had not allowed him to stay near me. No visits; they would be too much excitement for me they told him, but I knew that he needed me.

So I crept to my luzo in the middle of the night. With a soft creak, the door opened, and I slipped into the huge hall that opened from the hallway to my room. Apparently, they had placed me in the sanctuary again, but this time not in a cell, but instead in a room that they used for the sick. Velvety moonlight flooded the room.

Parilar slept in a corner way in the back where pillows and blankets were piled up into a sleeping place as soft as clouds.

Gently, I stroked his soft fur. He snored away quietly, and now and then, the tip of his tail twitched back and forth. He, too, appeared to be still exhausted from the battles, because otherwise he would have been awakened by my presence.

I remained sitting beside him until the moon grew pale and the dawn immersed the hall in a diffuse light. Against my will, I left Parilar and smuggled myself back into my room, where I slept away the entire next day.

The next night I awoke again and crept through my room to the door. Energetically, I rattled the door knob, but it wouldn't open. Darn! Who had locked my door? And why? It was certainly the guards who had found out that I had secretly visited Parilar and wanted to put an end to that.

Muttering, I crossed my arms and sat down on my bed again. When could I see Parilar again?

I fell back asleep. It was already light outside when I was awaked by clanging keys, and the door opened with a creak. In came Catleya, Lacato, Fanres, Lauren, Fedor, Sagor and, to my surprise – Zaron!

They all grinned at me expectantly, even Zaron. I just stared back foolishly. What were they all doing here?

After a "one, two, three," my mother started them all singing:

"HAPPY BIRTHDAY TO YOU, HAPPY BIRTHDAY TO YOU, HAPPY BIRTHDAY, DEAR JELLA, HAPPY BIRTHDAY TO YOU!!!"

I just looked at them taken aback and couldn't grasp it. Today was my birthday? On December 2nd? All these years I hadn't known and now .... I no longer knew what I should think. Luckily my mother freed me from this embarrassing situation and pressed a moist kiss on my cheek.

"Jella, today is your birthday. When I gave you to the Capuchs, I kept your birth date a secret because I absolutely wanted to protect you from Gribor. If he had found out that you were born under Saturn, he might have lured you here sooner, and you would have been easier prey for him. I thought Gribor would most likely start searching for you here, if he found out that you existed..."

That sounded logical. I forgave her right away for just finding out about my birthdate so many years later.

Startled, I opened my eyes wide. "Then I am now sixteen years old!" I cried out.

Everyone laughed.

Fanres took me in his arms and patted my back awkwardly. Lacato hugged me and congratulated me, chuckling; Fedor grinned impudently and squeezed me in a friendly way. Sagor and Lauren did the same.

Zaron bowed, which was then embarrassing for me. Then he donned a dignified expression and started a speech, "Of course, you should not celebrate your sixteenth without gifts. That is a meaningful age! In our village one is an adult at sixteen. And with that, you have earned a special gift. You can come in!" shouted Zaron through the open door.

170

I couldn't believe my eyes when I saw Parilar, whom I still thought was deathly ill, with a red gift bow around his neck.

"A red bow for a boy cat! My goodness, what have they done to you?"

But apparently he had thought up the joke on his own, because he winked at me mischievously. What a beast! Always out for pranks. He looked recovered, even if he still seemed a bit battered.

"Parilar!" I dashed to him and wrapped my arms around his neck. "You are healthy again!"

He croaked out a tired "Happy Birthday" and snorted good-naturedly.

"I had to lock the door of your room so you wouldn't slip out to him again last night. Parilar needed rest, even if you did successfully save him. It was supposed to be a special surprise. Follow us outside; something is waiting for you there!"

Catleya pulled me by the arm, and I was only able to quickly slip into my shoes before she had already pulled me to the door. We went slowly across the square in the direction of the training grounds and crossed them.

"Fanres, the cloth"! Lacato commanded and quickly tied a black cloth over my eyes.

"Hey, this really will not do!" I tried to pull the cloth from my eyes again, but now Lacato held my hands down. Being touched by Lacato wasn't really all that bad for me, and I struggled mostly for show. We climbed a small hill, and then I had to stop dead.

"Ready?" Lacato asked.

I nodded involuntarily. The cloth was removed from eyes!

"That is yours!" I heard Zaron's voice. "That is a gift from the village to you because you rescued us from a great danger and saved us from slavery."

"Oh, my God!" I cried out.

"You are out of your minds! I can't believe it!" I leaped for joy. If I hadn't been so tired, I would have done a handspring, I was so excited.

In front of me stood a brand-new wooden house. The villagers must have hastily built it in the past few days. They wanted to show me that I belonged with them and that they wanted to keep me here! I rejoiced inside. It was more like a little house, but it was a very beautiful little house. It was located at the foot of the little hill and the outside was painted off-white with a lime solution. It smelled like fresh paint; it wasn't yet dry.

A small set of steps out of light-colored wood led to the door. Nothing could hold me back now. I made a beeline into my own little realm. First I saw the little hallway, ran into the kitchen, and then marveled at the generous bathroom with a wooden tub and the wonderfully cozy living room. A soft light-colored carpet was laid out, and next to the fur-covered settee was a soft bed for Parilar. A wall of windows gave me a wonderful view of the broad landscape. My bedroom was fashioned almost like my old room at the Capuchs'. With blue walls and a wonderful bed.

"We knew that you loved your room at the Capuchs', so we didn't want to change too much," Catleya winked at me.

Enthusiastically I hopped from one foot to the other. All of this was so unbelievable. My first house of my own! I already felt at home before I had even moved in.

"Do you like it? You could stay forever and live here." Fanres and Zaron looked at me quizzically.

"It is...perfect! Thanks so much, that is so-" I broke off.

"But if I were to stay here, what about Rose? I must look for her because Gribor will have hidden her so that she cannot free herself. And my school? How will it continue in the other world?"

I was much too confused to be able to so suddenly grasp how much my life had changed.

"You must decide! Between staying here and going back to the world in which you spent years in the past. As to Rose's hiding place, we believe that it is located in this world. So it could be better to search from here. I believe Catleya has news for you regarding that." Zaron looked me straight in the eye.

"What kind of news?" Only now did it occur to me that I hadn't spoken to Catleya since the morning after the battle. Had she found something out? I looked at her with big eyes, "Did you find something out?"

"Perhaps there is a trail, but I am not sure," she returned in a serious voice.

"On the evening of the battle, I was on the way back with Jali when I saw something blinking in the mountains far away to the east. That made me curious, and we turned off in this direction.

"This area is completely uninhabited, and I first had a suspicion that a further group of trolls was advancing. I circled a while over the place that we

172

hadn't reached until the middle of the night, but couldn't recognize anything. Until Jali suddenly dove.

"There was a cave entrance below. We couldn't see anyone, so we crept in carefully on all fours. After a few minutes, we discovered the light of a lantern. I was completely surprised when I recognized Beleia, who was searching the grotto with a lantern. It had been the light of this lantern that we had seen from afar.

"She was scared to death by my sudden appearance and only after she had calmed down again, did she explain her strange behavior.

"A few days ago she had set out to get herself a supply of herbs and medicinal substances for the winter. She does that every fall because the healing power of the plants is strongest then. In the process, she came across a strange trail several days ago, still before the battle. There were three people and a huge luzo, as she could see from the footprints that had moved up the mountain. The luzo was none of ours; she could see that from the impression of the paws.

"On the way, she sensed an aura that Gribor had left behind. One of the trails was made by a child; it was small footprints in shoes that do not belong to our world, she said. She could not categorize the third footprint. If Gribor and a child with strange shoes had appeared in the vicinity two days before the attack, it can perhaps have been Rose. The trail ended in the cave.

"When she arrived there, it was empty and looked as if no one had ever been inside. I believe that this could be a first clue of Rose. Maybe they rested there, and Gribor then went further with them.

"Jali and I still flew around several more hours to find a trail, but the area there is devoid of people to the last corner. And no luzos were to be found; Jali surely would have noticed them from far away."

The thoughts in my head came thick and fast and I was tongue-tied.

"Jella, I am certain that there is more of a possibility of finding Rose here than in the other world. Here we have a trail and Jali and I will help you and continue to collect information. Gribor is surely dead; he can no longer lead us to her, but we can try to pick up his old trail."

I swallowed hard. "All right, I'll stay here, but I would still like to say goodbye to everyone in my old home."

My mother smiled gently. "Of course, in a few days you can fly off when you and Parilar are completely normal again."

Lacato's Gift

We spent the rest of the day in my house and had a good time. The villagers had even thought of filling the pantry, making it easier for me to make a final decision in favor of their village. Not until it had already become dark outside did my new guests take their leave.

Only Lacato stayed. We sat in the living room and had left the huge door to the veranda open. Countless stars shone in the black night sky. A cold breeze blew in on us unpleasantly, and I fished the blanket from the sofa.

"Do you often think about Lesla?" I interrupted the silence.

He winced. "Yes, I wish it hadn't happened that way."

Sadly, I agreed with him. I missed Lesla, too, and I still felt partly responsible for her death. The 'Great Five' no longer existed without her either. Who would come to us as the last of the Great Five and take Lesla's place?

As if Lacato had read my thoughts, he said, "I wonder who will be chosen as the last of the Great Five. Do you have any idea?"

Clueless, I shook my head. "I haven't the foggiest notion. It's a shame that part of the Codices was torn. Maybe the answer was in there," I commented.

Stunned, Lacato looked at me. "You don't know yet?"

"What don't I know?" I asked curiously.

"The first part is no longer in two. I patched it together!"

"What do you mean?"

He grinned. It was as quiet as a mouse.

Impatiently I poked him in the side and laughed, "Tell me already, you secret monger!"

He kept me in suspense a few more seconds to torture me before he finally spit out the words.

"I have found my talent!"

What had he just said? He had found his talent? I looked at him with wide eyes.

"Don't look at me like that. You heard me right. I have found my talent! I can repair objects and change them back. Look here!"

He stood up, looked around the room and took a small iron candleholder from the coffee table. Ruthlessly, he bent it with all his might into an ugly curve.

"Are you crazy?" I shouted and jumped next to him.

Effortlessly, the strong guy pushed me away again and let me know with his expression that I should be still; Then he stroked the metal carefully with two fingers, murmured a few words in a strange language and to my astonishment, the candle holder bent back into its original shape.

Stunned, I stared at the item. "Wow, truly impressive!"

Lacato shook off the praise with a hand gesture and then yawned heartily. "I believe I have to go to bed. It's been several nights since I slept at all...!"

"But hopefully not because of me and all this?" I joked and made and sweeping arm movement.

Lacato grinned and shook his head. "You'd like that, wouldn't you?" He packed his things and left after hugging me goodbye.

I would have liked to have kept him with me, but then I remembered Lesla. She and Lacato had been in love.

Only now did I notice how exhausted I still was. I had to go to bed.

During the night, I dreamed about Lacato. One time when I woke up, I regretted not having him nearby. Somewhere in my stomach a few butterflies woke up. The next time Lacato visited, I swore to myself that I wouldn't be so tired. Anyway, I was an adult in Tyrsenor. With a smile on my lips, I fell asleep again.

Decisions

I blinked and then tore open my eyes, frightened. Where was I?

From my bed I could look out the big window to the wide plain that surrounded the village, and slowly, the memories of my birthday celebration yesterday came back into my mind. I had spent the first night in my new house!

During the night I had dreamt, and all I could remember was that it would come true. Unfortunately, I couldn't remember the content any longer.

Sighing, I got myself up and shuffled into the kitchen to first make myself a strong cup of tea. I slowly swallowed the bitter hot liquid and suppressed a shudder. Now I was finally awake.

Curious, I then inspected my well-filled wardrobe, which boasted many new articles of clothing. Some came from my time with the Capuchs; others my mother must have bought new. Parilar appeared to have been underway with Catleya often in the past few days in spite of his exhaustion...

Hurriedly, I put on a simple black long-sleeved shirt and a pair of pants along with black boots. In front of the door, an icy wind swept against me and I ran back to quickly get a fur jacket.

When I went out again, Fanres suddenly stood in front of the entrance and asked me to come to Zaron, who wanted to speak to me.

I had never been in Zaron's house, which was surely the oldest of all the houses and huts in the village. It looked clean and well cared for. In the vestibule, flowers stood on a cabinet and the windows were decorated with embroidered curtains.

When I had entered, a woman came down the stairs to the upper floor. She was tall and slender; she had tied her gray hair into a bun at the back of her head, which made her look older that she probably was. I estimated she was more than fifty years old; perhaps she was even older.

"You must be Jella," she spoke in a friendly, rasping voice and extended her hand.

I nodded in embarrassment, because she made a strong, noble impression on me, and I politely shook her hand in greeting.

"I am Zaron's wife, call me Gerla," she explained to me.

"We spoke about you yesterday for a long time and have a request for you. Come into the parlor; then we will discuss everything."

I was now more uncertain that before. What did Zaron have planned? He sat in a large room whose dark wooden ceiling was supported by beams just as dark. His carved armchair stood at the head of an enormously wide and long table.

Next to him at the corner sat the older man with the gray beard who had put Zaron in his place a few days ago and cleared the way for saving the village.

Both greeted me cordially and asked me to take a seat.

Zaron's older follower introduced himself as Elohi. I now learned that he was the village blacksmith. Gerla sat next to me on a wooden chair and looked at her husband with a serious face.

He initially cleared his throat and spoke slowly at first, but then faster and faster, "We have conferred again in the past few days. The Council of Elders convened and discussed the situation," Zaron shared in a serious voice. All the while, he sat as stiff as a board on the edge of his seat.

What was wrong? Had they changed their minds? A fright traveled through all of my limbs, and I believe that I began to tremble.

"Now don't talk so haughtily," Gerla cut in. "You're scaring her. Get to the point and change your approach."

At the same time, she took my left hand and squeezed it gently, which calmed me right away. Because Elohi also smiled at me, I was more relaxed and then listened attentively to Zaron's flood of words.

Zaron cleared his throat again and continued in a husky voice, "All right, I admit that I treated you unjustly at first. I was not satisfied with Parilar's choice and didn't want to admit that his instinct was right. But it was a blessing that you came to us and helped us to heal the misfortune that destroyed the last generation of the Great Five and to build up a new generation. We are therefore happy, above all, because you had already been one of us..."

Gerla raised her eyes to the ceiling as if she wanted to say, "Get to the point!"

"Well...," Zaron lurched further through his speech, somewhat irritated by Gerla's annoyed looks, "...well, we wanted to ask you to continue to help us.

We need your further support because we are in a situation that is not very simple for the village."

Elohi moved his white-haired head slowly and thoughtfully up and down in agreement. The village blacksmith now took over the conversation, which apparently relieved Zaron because he leaned back in his chair, exhaling.

"We don't know much about the world outside of the mountains. For a long time it was no different there than it was with us, and we had never felt the need to have contact there. Because of that and because only few luzos can pass through the time tunnel, we lost our knowledge about the other world. It appeared just as unchanging to us as ours. That world was, however, so full of war and hardship that we no longer wanted to know about it; it appeared to be lost.

"Only through a coincidence was a luzo rider in the other world many decades ago, after we had been out of contact with it for many centuries. When he returned, he reported astonishing things. That part of the globe had completely changed. It had become as you know it, with self-propelled coaches, flying machines and terrible weapons, much luxury and prosperity, but also without magic and without mythical beings, who were all driven out." He paused.

"But in this world, there were descendants of our magician, who called themselves scientists. They even found mathematical formulas with which they could describe how our luzos managed to negotiate the barrier! They collected astonishing knowledge and when we learned that, we saw the danger that one day the luzos would be exposed. Hard to conceive what will happen if Tyrsenor were discovered."

Elohi had narrowed his eyes; he was so appalled by this idea.

"Therefore we decided to send messengers there, who were supposed to study this knowledge and bring us up to date. Unfortunately these messengers seldom returned and eventually stayed there completely. Why, we don't know. So we are only able to know after a fashion how far that world has developed. That worries us. We are afraid of discovery and new attempts to oppress us."

Now Gerla began to speak. "Jella, you and Catleya are the only ones who ever had the desire to return to us from over there. We have gained trust in you. Therefore we are asking you to go to school there again, to graduate and then to study so that we can learn how the world is developing and what we must do to continue to be protected."

All three looked at me eagerly.

I initially thought "If that's all it is," but then made a long face. What had Zaron said on my birthday, "At sixteen women here are adults."?

Somehow I had imagined that I could now do and not do whatever I wanted; with Parilar and the other three – perhaps soon to be four – roam about the whole day and enjoy life. Besides, I had to look for Rose; that was much more important.

Gerla had possibly seen through me because she said in a serious voice, "Becoming an adult here as well as there means that one has duties and contributes to the community. You would soon be asked to take on a task, perhaps procuring food or extracting medicinal substances from herbs, teaching in school or something else. Catleya has already hinted that you could even take over Beleia's place as healer if you learn to read the Codices, for which you would need to study ancient languages. Even the Great Five are not constantly at the training grounds; each of them pursues a career after the training.

"But we here need the knowledge that you have already acquired and which is called science there. We fear that our magic will not be strong enough to stop the influences of the other world. Concerning Rose, we have sent out luzos under Catleya's leadership to look up the trail. You don't know your way around here and would be hopelessly lost. Because of that, you can confidently leave the search to us."

I looked at the ground and tried to sort out my feelings. It became clear to me that she was right. I couldn't be on vacation here for the rest of my life. For the time being, the search for Rose was better off in my mother's hands.

I now felt great peace and clarity inside of me. My task was set. I was an adult and had to take on responsibility. That consisted of understanding the knowledge of the other world and using it for us, for my community. And using it to protect Tyrsenor from dangers.

The last attack had come from inside of the village, from Gribor. But he already had made use of resources from the other world. Now we had to prevent the existence of Tyrsenor from becoming exposed. That was my task; only I was presently in a position to acquire the necessary knowledge.

When I looked up, I looked into eager, serious faces.

I nodded. Gerla squeezed my hand, and I saw a tear running down her cheek.

In addition, that meant that I would be able to intensify my search for Rose because I would be at home in both worlds.

Return to Hokksund

After the conversation at Zaron's, I went through the village for a round of greetings, getting to know more inhabitants, but only superficially because Parilar didn't stay put anywhere for a long time. Then I finally made my way with my luzo to Villa Capuch in Hokksund, my old home.

Having arrived there, I first climbed the entrance steps and opened the house door. Carin and Per sat in the living room and looked as if it had been nothing. Camilla was not with them.

"Hi!" I said and after I was greeted with only a brief nod, I went up the stairs.

I opened the door to Camilla's room and a gust of sweet perfume reached my nostrils.

"Out!" she screamed and a pink towel barely missed me.

"I just wanted to say goodbye!"

As was to be anticipated, she didn't ask anything, but instead just screeched, "Yes, ciao!" Then she slammed the door shut in my face. Fortunately, I was no longer stuck with her.

I went down the steps and proceeded to Per and Carin.

"I wanted to say goodbye. From today on, I will be living with the luzos..."

Both of them blinked at me dispassionately. Then Carin began, "All right, goodbye."

That was all.

Per shot me an unreadable look. "I withdrew you from school after we couldn't reach you for a few days. Here is your diploma." With that he pressed a few sheets of paper into my hands.

"Goodbye."

I had a scare: I was supposed to continue going to school! What was I supposed to do now? The question remained open. Per didn't want to talk to me about it.

I did want to get one question out of the way, "Did you ever hear anything from the police? Did any news of Rose surface?"

Per looked around briefly and when Carin didn't react, he took me by the arm and pushed me across the hallway into his study.

"This hypocritical person, Mrs. Turgel, was here one more time and asked about you. I told her that you were on a visit to another school. She then shared with me that no trace of Rose was to be found. This ominous Nathan never turned up. They will continue to look for a period of time, but sooner or later they will then have to give up."

He looked at me penetratingly, "Jella, I am certain that you are the only one here who is able to find a trail."

With that, he turned around and left me standing. I didn't know what to think of that and decided to now leave the villa for good. When the door clicked shut, I turned for a last time toward the house in which I had lived so long. I had never considered it my home.

Next, I knocked on the door of Drude and Hakan.

"Jella, you haven't visited us in so long. How are you? It is really nice of you to come by."

Drude's wrinkled face beamed at me, and the thousands of tiny wrinkles were amplified when she smiled.

"Hi, Grandma!" I took her in my arms and hugged her long and hard. Then, however, I began to sputter, "I am coming by for the last time now. From now on, I will be living somewhere else. I have finally found some place where I like living."

Already, her wise eyes were shadowed, but she nodded sympathetically. She simply said, "Let's talk."

And we laughed and talked for many hours. By the time I left Drude and Hakan, I had found out things that surprised me. So much had become clear: They had been in contact with Tyrsenor a long time ago and had much knowledge about prior events.

I had only received inklings about many things. But it was enough to rouse my astonishment and make me curious. I planned to visit them again in a few months and then learn more.

Toward evening, I headed for Rose's mother. I wanted to speak with her, perhaps encourage her.

I still didn't know what I should say. The whole truth? That was completely impossible; she wouldn't believe a word and besides, I was not permitted to speak about it because I would betray the secret of my new home by doing so.

When I pushed the shabby doorbell of Rose's apartment, Rose's brother Oskar opened the door.

"Hey, kiddo. How are you?" I asked in a husky voice. This visit was the most difficult; I clearly sensed that now.

"Jella!" he cried joyfully and clung to my leg. "Where have you been for so long?"

I smiled sadly. "I had a lot on my plate." That was a major understatement...

"Is your mom here, too?"

"Of course, she is in the living room," he answered. I tousled his hair one more time and then knocked cautiously on the door. When I entered, Rose's mother jumped up and flung her arms around my neck.

"Jella! Where were you? For so long, every time I called you, the Capuchs said that you were away for a long time. I was so worried."

I smiled, heavy-hearted. She was worried about me although her daughter had disappeared.

"Come to me, sit down next to me," she said with a warm smile.

"Tell me, where you have been."

I wasn't prepared for that. I had sooner expected her to tell me about her search for Rose. I hemmed and hawed and then said that I had been looking for a new school and would likely be moving away. Nothing else occurred to me at the moment. Then I asked if there were anything new, perhaps information about Rose? The question was hypocritical, I knew that, but I wanted to change the topic to Rose.

"No," said her mother, now deeply saddened. "You didn't hear anything either?"

I pressed my lips together and shook my head.

"Will you come again another time?" she then also asked.

"Maybe in a few years; I really don't know," I said through a veil of tears.

She took me in her arms and with sad thoughts of Rose, we sat next to one another for a few minutes without speaking.

Then Rose's mother brought me to the door for the last time.

"Goodbye," she breathed.

"You, too," I managed to utter between pinched lips; then she shut the door. Now I really began to sob. We both missed Rose so much.

I also knew that I had made the right decision. I would come again; I would go to school daily, but no longer in Hokksund. So my departure was final. It happened like this:

When I was with my adopted grandparents, Drude nudged me mischievously when I worriedly showed her my final report card. I didn't know how I was now supposed to fulfill the promise I had given Zaron."

"Look at it," she said giggling.

Only now did I notice that the second sheet was a letter from another school. It was the acceptance in the senior classes of a first-class high school in Oslo. Drude was the one who had made sure that I didn't have to return with empty hands. After Per had pressed the final grade report into my hands, I was convinced that I wouldn't be able to keep my promise to Tyrsenor's council by continuing to attend school.

My concern about how I would tell Zaron was as if blown away. Teetering somewhere between laughing and crying, I hugged Drude and left this familiar house.

I called Parilar, and at this moment, I saw a single snowflake dancing in the darkness of the sky.

The Great Five are complete

Fanres was already at the training grounds and ran excitedly toward me when he saw me coming.

"I must report the most important news to you as quickly as possible, because you must be aware of it before the time comes: Early tomorrow, the last of the Great Five will be chosen!" he reported, excited.

Astonished, I looked into his ice blue eyes. "What? Do we already know who it is?"

"No, but we have found a luzo that senses a bond. To a human. We know that it will choose its rider today."

After all the days of recuperation and the farewell scenes today, I felt like I had to move. I wanted to fight! Together, we strode to our customary training location, and Fanres tossed me a sword.

"Attack!" I cried with a feigned war cry.

Fanres ran with his loudly droning laugh into the battle. At the end, we both lay on the ground, gasping for air and panting competitively.

"For me, team-Fanres and team-Jella have fought to a tie," I panted.

"Yes, apparently. But there will be revenge; however, rest now and come to me tomorrow before sunrise. Then we will go to the ceremony together."

The next morning, I pried myself out of bed while it was still dark and with a sleepy Parilar, went to Fanres. His luzo came along, too, and as a foursome, we joined the already assembled villagers. I took my place next to Lauren and Fedor.

The ceremony began with Zaron mounting the platform with sedate steps. In both hands, he carried a bowl filled with Landuza water. It was the same ceremony as at my arrival in the village many weeks ago. It seemed to me as if an eternity had passed since then.

Behind him padded a luzo unfamiliar to me, whose fur shimmered in a pale rust. Curiously, it eyed those gathered around and bowed briefly in our direction.

"That is Minula," whispered Fedor in my ear.

Now Zaron sprinkled the new luzo with the holy water and said a few words to her. All at once, it was deathly quiet on the square and it appeared as if time stood still when Minula came down, crept around those gathered and sniffed with concentration.

Finally she stopped in front of a slouching red-haired boy. She appeared to make contact to something. Then the boy shyly stretched out his hand to Minula, who good-naturedly snorted.

The crowd cheered and Zaron came toward them with the water and beamed his smile at them.

"So he can laugh," I thought mischievously.

He led the boy and Minula back to the platform together and repeated the same ritual which Parilar and I had undergone. Their forehead and snout glistened gold, too. When they, too, were drizzled with the water and the cheering had subsided, number five and his luzo came toward us, the other four, who now stood together to receive our new and final comrade.

"I am Samuel." He looked each of us in the eyes and when his gaze met mine, I smiled at him encouragingly.

He shyly answered my smile and I immediately felt a profound sympathy for his freckled face with the stub nose.

Then we formed a circle and all five of us hugged.

We were one!

Now the silence on the square gave way to a tumultuous cheer and we were surrounded by celebrating villagers, who alternately shook our hands, clapped us on the back or lifted us up. Now we were finally complete:

Number one: Lacato, the eldest

Number two: Lauren the laughing one

Number three, Fedor, the daredevil

Number four: Jella, the responsible one

Number five: Sam, the gentle one

We rose up into the air with our luzos and all the other riders did the same. All cheered; countless luzos with their riders flew with us across the already dark sky. I glimpsed Catleya on Jali's back and waved at her vigorously. Laughing, she returned my gesture, as a familiar voice drew my attention.

"Hi, Jell-O!" Lacato flew next to me on his powerful luzo. "Up for a race?"

Challengingly, he looked at me. I stood up to his gaze.

"You might as well already admit your defeat now!" I cried and Parilar shot off.

We had to be careful because Parilar and I had almost run into others due to the many luzos in the sky. To our delight, Lauren and Fedor joined in and after a few encouraging looks, Sam decided to follow, too.

In the beginning, Parilar and I were way out front, but to my surprise, Sam who had been holding back up to now, overtook us after a while. But at the end, Lacato of all people went past me and shot to the goal first. The next time I swore to myself that I would win.

There would be a next time. Because we were the Great Five again.

Note for experts on Norway:

The readability of the text was more important to us than remaining true to detail in the description of the Norwegian landscape and the customs of the inhabitants.
So "Hamborgstrømskogen" was left out in favor of "Engermidtskogen" and the latter again shortened to "Engerskogen". That reads more fluidly.
In the form of address we Americanized.
That also applies to the designations for the police, because hardly anyone in this country would identify a policeman with "Politiførstebetjent."
If something else should occur to someone, we are always thankful for advice.